DARK NEED

A DARK DESIRE NOVEL

J THOMPSON

Created with Vellum

ABOUT THE BOOK

Dark Desire
Addicted to Desire, Tainted by Love

Constance

Abandoned as a baby, Constance has spent all her life alone, surviving from day-to-day and dealing with her ever-increasing hunger. Since the age of 18, she has fought the need for sex until she can't take it anymore and finally relinquishes her innocence. Five years on, she spends her week-days as an office clerk in Hackney, London, and her weekends searching for nameless hook-ups in the hope they will quench her unrelenting desires and her body's constant need. A freak accident sets her on a course that changes her life completely but finally reveals who she truly is.

Dominic

An enforcer for his kind, Dominic's job is to protect Succubi's from other immortal races and hide them from the humans. His job simple, until a rogue female hits his radar and sets off every protective instinct he has. He can't help but find her body alluring, releasing a desire he is not ready for. But Dominic's life is turned upside down when her soul calls to him, sealing a bond that is forbidden.

1

Reality versus Fantasy

THE FIRST TIME CONSTANCE SAW HIM, HER HEART STOPPED for a second and then restarted at a thunderous pace. She could have sworn he could hear it from the other side of the room. Since that night, and every night since, she had ventured into the bar and reacted in the exact same way to his presence.

Constance had no idea who he was, only that, on some level, he called to her as she watched him, taking in his every movement until he would leave. In some way, she was a stalker, obsessed with a man who didn't know she existed. He was gorgeous, tall, and built just how she now preferred her men. Or she would if she stuck to one type.

From her favourite seat by the bar, she had been able—on every occasion—to look at him unhindered. Stalking would probably be a more apt word for her new hobby. He would tower over her small five-feet-four frame if he was standing in front of her. His shoulders made most rugby players look weak, and his appeal only increased when you took in the chin-length dark hair and intense green eyes set below a forbidding pair of eyebrows. A nose that was a little crooked and sinful lips finished the entire package off. A package that Constance fantasised about on a regular occurrence.

The man sizzled with intensity and made blood rush to everywhere but her brain when she saw him. But that's about as far as it got. She was too chicken to approach him, and the fear of rejection held her firmly on her stool each time. Instead, she focused on the men she could, in short... pull.

Constance's weekly trips to the bar weren't just for the peep show. She ventured there for one purpose:

Sex.

No, she didn't do it at the bar, but she went to acquire a partner she hoped would help take the edge off the craving she had been suffering with for the past six months. Though *craving* would be a tame word for what she suffered from: need, nothing like she had ever felt before. The need to release but being unable to do so. Every weekend, and sometimes midweek, Constance would come to the bar and seek out a new partner in the hopes they could do what the previous hadn't. Yet, after six months, she was still no closer to that elusive orgasm. Instead, they left her dancing along the ledge, the drop to oblivion teasingly close yet so far out of reach.

She was in an unfulfilled purgatory with only the fantasy images of Mr. Tall, Dark and Gorgeous to prevent her from having a complete mental break down. A sure-fire way of getting her locked up would be to have a child-like tantrum over the fact she hadn't orgasmed in six months.

So here she was staring up at another white ceiling. This had become a regular occurrence; waking up in a stranger's bed after a night of doing the dirty. Constance turned her head, almost dreading to see her recent conquest wide awake, but luckily for her, his snores told her he was still out of it. And so he should be. She had literally ridden him till he had passed out, and still she could have gone on. That was her problem: no matter how many times she did it—yes, she was calling it 'it' in her head—the overwhelming need for completion eluded her. Once again, she had struck out and would remain edgy and no doubt grumpy for the rest of the day.

Constance had lost count of the men she'd slept with, and she didn't want to think about the amount too much, either. She didn't doubt that if you looked up *slapper* in the dictionary, there would probably be her picture right there next to the definition. It wasn't that she was addicted to sex; it was more trying out to see if she could find someone who would fix her. She wasn't normal. How could she be, when she was unable to orgasm?

She gave one final check to make sure Steve—or was it Mike?—was still asleep before she slid out of bed and collected her clothing from the floor.

Constance quickly slipped out of the bedroom and into the hallway, before she dressed and made it to the front door with no issues. This was how it went every week. She would wake up in someone else's bed, her needs unquenched, and she would escape before the guy had even stirred. But even this routine wasn't working anymore. It was leaving her desperate and emotional.

Constance made it out of the front door and into the street with not a peep from the sleeping lover. She headed down the road in an attempt to not look like she was yet again doing the 'walk of shame'.

Without looking back, Constance lifted up the hood of

her jacket and pulled out the headphones she had stashed in her pocket. With quick steps she headed towards the nearest tube station. It was still early, so there weren't many people milling about. The bonus of living in London meant a route home was always close by, and, luckily, where she had ended up the night before meant she was only one stop away from being home.

Head down and Oyster card in hand, Constance quickly made it through the ticket barriers of the tube station and down to platform to wait for the next train to Hackney. She let the deep, low tones of Evanescence fill her head as she fought tiredness from the full night of sex, which, coupled with the storm in her stomach from her unquenched desires, meant she would not be resting well today.

Constance shuddered and tried to supress the need to rub her arms. She felt cheap and dirty inside. But she didn't know how else she was supposed to deal with her addiction —well, that's what she thought it was. She possibly could attend a sex addicts group, but she doubted that would deal with her body's need.

A slight tingle up her neck pulled Constance from the screen of her phone. She looked up and to the right just as the ruggedly handsome man she had been stalking at the bar walked past. Constance fought the gasp that bubbled its way up her throat when, for the first time, his intense green eyes locked with her own.

Heat rushed through her veins, like it always did, only this time the intensity of his gaze sent her blood boiling. The recent feeling of calm vanished, replaced by a wild need for this man's hands on her skin. She felt flushed, and she knew her cheeks were bright red. In an attempt to hide her obvious reaction, Constance reluctantly pulled her eyes away and bent her head. She pulled in deep breaths as she fought to control herself. She was like a slave to her body's needs, and if she could have, she would have followed that man and begged him to ease her pain.

Constance watched him as he moved away from the corner of her eye, before the arrival of her train pulled her focus and gave her time to breathe. She pushed past the other passengers and made her way to a corner, where she sat down and closed her eyes.

If she had liked him before, that feeling had increased tenfold now. He had looked at her and moved past almost close enough to touch. His scent had invaded her senses. Her fantasies would be on a whole new level—but that's all they could be. No man who looked and smelled like that would be interested in a woman who slutted herself out for an elusive orgasm.

No, that man there was out of her league, and it was about time she accepted as much and got him out of her head.

2

_____

With my green eyes

DOMINIC WATCHED THE TRAIN AS IT PULLED AWAY AND OUT OF sight. He frowned as he curbed his body's reactions and moved towards the end of the platform to where his fellow enforcer and member of the Alpha team had departed the long-gone train.

He had seen that female before—how could he not; she was breathtakingly beautiful. She had been in the bar every weekend for a while now and always sat on the end stool. Dominic smirked to himself as he recalled her reaction to him when he had deliberately walked past her. Her gasp and heated cheeks had proved she wasn't just watching him in the bar for shits and giggles. No, that female was very much interested, and he would bet anything she would be very much open to his advances.

But he wouldn't go there—couldn't go there. She was human, and his kind didn't dally with the mortals.

Although, sometimes they would all make the exception. Most of the enforcers were into bedding mortals, but Dom found he just couldn't stomach the idea. Dominic attempted to put the female out of his mind as he met with the closest thing he had to a brother.

Sebastian was an enforcer for the succubi, like him, and his second in command of the Alpha team. Sebastian was old school, as he liked to put it. His long brown hair was always tied back, and he was always dressed impeccably, even when in the middle of a fight. Sebastian was the only member of the enforcers to have been bonded, by evidence of the dark, black bond marks on his hands. His mate was gone though, taken from him not long after they had bonded. The loss had sent his friend into a downward spiral of self-destruction. One that had taken the entire Alpha team to help bring him out of. Now, he was the controlled one, the one who thought of everything logically and with a detachment Dominic wished he could emulate.

But that didn't make Sebastian any less deadly. He could deliver retribution with more venom than the rest of them. Only recently Sebastian had delivered justice to a male who had not only captured a succubi female, but had tortured and done tests on her in a hidden facility. The male deserved every ounce of pain he had received. Sebastian's only wish had been that the male had been immortal, so he could have gone through the pain over and over again.

Luckily, they had saved the female in time, and Callum, another member of the alpha team, had been able to bring his bonded back from the brink of death. That being the positive, the alpha team, minus Callum, had been charged with hunting down the facilities like the one they had raided and making sure there wasn't anything or anyone left. So far, in the past month they had taken out a further three, managing to free three vampyres, two werewolves and a dark fae. Most of the other victims had been human and had not survived.

So here he was, trolling the tube stations for a hint of any information, as ordered by Michael, the self-appointed leader of the succubi council. Just the thought of that male made Dominic's left eye twitch. If anyone was more unsuited to ruling a race, it was Michael.

There had been a royal house that ruled and guided his race, only in one night, they had been wiped out. The queen's consort, one of Dominic's mentors, had been brutally killed in a raid. Upon hearing the news of her male's death, the queen became inconsolable. They had been bonded so strongly that his death had meant her own. There had been a child, only she had vanished that night, leaving the succubi race leaderless.

Michael had always been an ambitious male and had used the opportunity to gain power. It was his idea that males and females—instead of being chosen and bonded young like tradition—were now only paired based on bloodlines.

Dominic sneered. That was Michael's way of purging the bloodlines. It also meant Dominic would never be chosen to have a mate of his own. He was a half-breed succubi, only he wasn't sure what his other half was—his mother had never divulged that information. But that hadn't stopped him, stopped him from being the best. The best at protecting his race, battle now was what he knew, what he craved.

"Dom, you with me?"

"Huh?" Dominic questioned as he realised Sebastian was talking to him.

"I said, have you found anything? All my leads so far have been useless." Their steps echoed in the near empty station as they headed for a non-descript door. One that would lead them topside and out of the view of the humans.

"No, nothing. Although the stench of vamp has been hard to miss."

"Hmm, strange that they should be making their whereabouts known," Sebastian growled out, letting his distaste be known. Dominic had no love for the leeches either—well, other than the love for splitting them in half and watching their blood turn to dust.

"Yes, I agree." Dom nodded as they passed through the door and into a stairwell. Multiple flights of stairs stretched above, leading them back up to the streets of London.

"I'm finding it harder to seek out my contacts. It's like they have gone to ground, like they are scared of something," Dominic admitted. "The atmosphere has changed; it's thick—" Dom stopped and looked his friend in the eye. "Like something big is about to drop."

Sebastian looked back at him and simply nodded. "Your gut-feeling has never led us wrong, Dom. Let's pray whatever it is, it's something we can handle, yes?"

"Yes, agreed. Come, let's get back. Michael will want his report." Dominic sneered as he started to climb the stairs. Although his thoughts were not on Michael. For some reason, they kept returning back to the bright blue eyes of the female.

3

The need is great

NUMBER 23. THE WHITE NUMBERS ON THE PLAIN, BLACK DOOR beckoned Constance, calling her home to her small apartment. This was the only place she felt remotely welcome. It was simply furnished, consisting of a small kitchen which was open-plan and made up the lounge also. It also had a tiny bathroom, and her bedroom. It was small, but cosy and cheap—if you could call London prices cheap.

As she opened the door and stepped inside, she released a long sigh. Her body ached. Being constantly aroused was exhausting, and having spent most of the night going at it, you would think Constance was ready to just relax.

But no—not her body. Since she had seen the green-eyed stranger at the tube station, her libido had been firing on all twelve cylinders. Even though her body thrummed again with the need to find some sort of release, she ignored it. The last time she had given in, it had made the entire situation worse. The stress of being unable to release, and being full of pent up need, was starting to take its toll on

Constance. She could barely sleep, her dreams always taking the erotic route, and eating had started to become a chore—forcing down a meal just so she would pass out was now the norm.

Constance was in a bad way, but what could she do? She couldn't go to her mother. No, that was not happening. Her mother was barely in the land of the sane anymore. When Constance was fifteen, her mother had been admitted to St Joseph's—a mental institution on the outskirts of London—and Constance was put into the system, being passed from one home to another and basically abandoned.

No one seemed to want a fifteen-year-old with issues, so as soon as she turned eighteen, Constance got herself a job and a place to live. Yes, she visited her mother, but those visits usually ended up with both of them crying for different reasons. She made no sense anymore, so asking her about Constance's current issue just wasn't worth the emotional hassle.

"We have had numerous complaints," the dark-haired woman started to say as she looked at Constnace's mother, who, as usual, was sat in her armchair in the lounge. Her hair, which Constance had managed to brush quickly, was greasy and lank. Her mother was barely with it. She would spend days not eating or drinking, and getting her to wash had become almost impossible. Constance had given up trying to force her mother to do anything. All that got her were slaps and shouting in her face.

Constance had been blamed for everything that went wrong in the past, only she didn't know why. If Constance was honest, she didn't know anything; who her father was; why they were alone in London, having to rely on foodbanks. Constance worked part-time at a restaurant as a dish washer, and that paid for what little they did have.

Since Constance was six, maybe seven, her mother had

become increasingly distant, falling in on herself and talking of strange things like monsters, murder and escape. If she looked back, she could honestly say her mother had never been the maternal type, either. Whenever she had cried, she'd just been glared at.

"Miss," the woman called out, and then looked to her colleague, frowning when Constance's mother ignored them. They both seemed nice enough, but there was a hardness about them that kept Constance back. They were both dressed casually, trying to act non-threatening. Constance wasn't fooled.

They had come for her mother. So now, as Constance sat on the sofa watching her mother start to rock back and forth, she knew she would be on her own. Only that didn't scare her as much as she thought it would. In fact, she felt relieved.

"Miss, we are here due to reports that you have been neglecting yourself and your daughter," the one who had introduced herself as Marie stated clearly. She smiled weakly at Constance before she stood and walked towards her mother. Kneeling in front of her, she tried to talk again.

"Miss?"

Only Constance knew what the response would be.

Quicker than any of them but Constance could comprehend, her mother lashed out, slapping the woman around the face before she started to scream.

"Monsters! Death—"

Constance closed her eyes and let the tears fall as her mother was subdued by the two women. Constance didn't stay to watch; she knew what they would do. Instead, she climbed the stairs to her small room and crawled onto the bed. Picking up a pillow, she placed it over her ears to block out the sound of her mother's screams.

They would take her away and she would be alone. She was better off alone.

Constance opened her eyes, not realising she had closed them. Reaching up, she felt a single tear had fallen, and she swiped it away. That day had been a blessing, a blessing for her and for her mother.

They had both been better off.

Her mother more so.

Constance thoughts returned to her issue.

There were the doctors, but what did she say? 'Hi, I'm Constance and I'm a sex addict who can't orgasm'? Yeah, that would go down well. Constance sighed heavily and threw herself down on the dingy small sofa.

Nope, she was on her own... this was something she would have to figure out and deal with herself. As much as she hated to, she would go out again tonight in the hopes she could find someone who could make everything better. Yes, she needed the sex, but the loneliness she had started to feel was now a hole in her chest, one that continued to get bigger.

Standing, Constance headed towards her bathroom. A long hot shower and a few hours' sleep, she hoped, would restore the small amount of positivity she had left. She had to keep going, even if she felt like the world could implode on her at any moment.

She couldn't give up... no matter what.

"What do you mean your contacts have vanished?" The high-pitched voice grated across Dominic's nerves. His fingers tightened, and he wished they were round the throat of the asshole producing the sound.

"I thought—I had assumed the Alpha team were the best. Obviously not." Michael looked down his nose at

Dominic. The councilman who had decided to take charge of the succubi race in the absence of a monarch was pushing his luck. The hate they had for each other was completely mutual. Dominic knew if Michael was given any excuse, Dom would be either banished or executed.

It would probably be the latter, Dominic thought. He kept his face blank as the councilman ranted about the Alpha team's apparent failings. There had been no failings as such. They had tracked down and destroyed five facilities where immortals were being punished. The fact that something bigger had driven his contacts underground was not a failing. It was a warning.

A warning that something big and bad was just around the corner. But Michael wouldn't see it like that—hell, the skinny bastard never ventured out into the mortal realm. Nope, he sat behind his minions and was happy to see everyone else do the dirty work.

"What do you plan to do about it, then, enforcer." Dominic looked blankly at the councilman on his perch, a raised seat sat above all.

"My lord, we shall continue the hunt. We still have a few leads to try out."

"Mmm, well go on, then. Don't bother coming back unless you have anything useful to say."

Dominic nodded once and turned. His booted footsteps echoed in the great hall. All the councilmen were quiet as he left the room. Not surprisingly, Sebastian was outside waiting as he emerged.

"So, what did he say?"

Dominic continued to walk, Sebastian falling into step beside him.

"The usual; the alpha team are useless, we are not to go back unless we have anything useful to say... Fucking prick.

Tell me again why I can't kill him? It would do the race a favour."

"Unless you plan on taking his place, Dom, I don't think that's a good idea. As much as he is a jumped-up little turd, he's keeping the race together and doing all the paperwork neither you nor I enjoy."

"Fuck. Yeah, forgot about that bit," Dominic laughed. No matter the job, the paperwork sucked.

"You going topside again?" Sebastian asked.

"Yeah, I have a few more informants to hunt down," Dominic admitted.

"You need back up?"

"I should be fine. Thank you, my friend." Dominic held his hand out, and Sebastian answered by grasping his forearm.

"Anytime. Just do me a favour."

"Anything."

"Avoid Pulse, will you." Sebastian looked Dominic in the eye, a serious expression on his face.

"And why? You know I like the vodka there."

"Vodka can be bought anywhere, and you know why. I've seen you watching her, Dom. She's human—mortal—which means a no go."

Dominic frowned. Surely he hadn't been that obvious in his watching of the female. But then again, Sebastian didn't miss a thing.

"Why, what's one mortal compared to another?"

"I have a feeling... that's all."

Slapping Sebastian on the back, Dominic moved past his lifelong friend. "You and your feelings... Don't worry, mother, I won't be late." Dominic laughed and moved towards the exit.

"I expect the Alphas to be training... just in case."

4

Foresight forewarned

CONSTANCE FELT EDGY. THAT WASN'T A NEW FEELING, BUT THE added extra of being unable to settle at all was certainly something she wasn't used to. Even the combination of a scalding hot shower, followed by a nap and a meal, hadn't helped.

The edginess was something she had spent years dealing with, but that, coupled with the new irritability, was already driving her mad. There had been a short period of time when she was younger where she would *sort herself out* in the hopes it would curb her issue. What girl failed to get sorted by a little battery power?

Turned out, she was one of the few who failed. Instead of helping her, it had made the entire situation worse. Constance had never been able to release, instead only hovering on the edge. Constance had also come to realise that it wasn't just the action and release her body craved, it was so much more. The connection, even a small one, when she was body to body with a man... it was that moment of touch that helped ease—if only slightly—the need that coursed through her constantly. The battery power had none of that, and, in fact, had sent her spiralling into a state where she was almost bedridden and in immeasurable pain. That had been a monumental learning curve for Constance, a lesson that had taught her quickly that as much as she wanted to, there was no way she could cheat and ignore her body's needs.

She was now its slave, and Constance hated it...

In fact, she loathed it.

But here she was, dressed in what she hoped was a seductive look. Tight, black jeans, white tank top, and her favourite push up bra, making the girls look a lot bigger than they actually were. Yes, it would be classed as false advertising, but she needed all the help she could get.

Her outfit, to her, was comfy and simple. She didn't do or ever had done fancy. As long as it helped show off what little assets she had, Constance was good. Keeping with the simple look, Constance finished it all off with braiding her long black hair into two French braids. Eyeliner and a hint of mascara helped make her blue eyes pop, and she was done.

Constance looked intently at her reflection in the mirror, turning from side to side before she picked up a deep maroon lipstick and placed it into her back pocket.

"Ugh, I guess you will do." Tucking an already loose strand of hair behind her left ear, Constance collected her small bag from the sofa and picked up her keys.

Doing one last check over her small home, she checked the lights were off and that it was tidy. If not, she would be worrying about it all evening. Her home was small, simple, and comfy. It was her way with dealing with her lonely life.

Blowing out a breath, Constance opened the door and

stepped out into the corridor. As usual she didn't linger, moving quickly towards the stairs, taking the multiple flights quickly. With a quick look to see if anyone was hanging about, she exited the building and headed for the main road.

Like most cities, there were good areas and not so good ones. Where Constance lived was on the borderline. It wasn't by choice—hell, Constance would love to live in one of those swanky, high-rise buildings that came with their own guard and gym. But when money was tight, you made do. London, after all, was a tad pricey.

Ignoring the cat-calls from a group of lads outside a pub on the corner of the road, she turned in the opposite direction. It sounded cliché and boring, but she would go where she always went:

Pulse.

This was her local, as well as being the place she felt the most comfortable. Constance was on first name terms with the bouncers there, so she always felt a little safer than if she went somewhere unknown. It was also the one place that should could guarantee she would see him. Mr. Green Eyes and Intense was also a regular. Her last reason was why she ventured out most nights. Constance had very little trouble picking up a willing partner for the evening. Why change a habit if it worked, right?

As Constance moved down the street, the irritability she had initially felt started to ease, even if only slightly. Instead, her body hummed with anticipation, as if it knew where she was going and what she would get out of the evening. Surprisingly, her steps felt lighter than they had earlier that day.

Feeling positive was something that didn't happen for her as of late, so she smiled and relished that small glimmer of hope that maybe tonight she would finally get some sort of relief.

She had to believe things could get better. She didn't know what she would do if they got worse.

Dominic rotated the small glass in his hand. The usually clear liquid changed slightly with each turn as the light reflected from the disco ball that spun lazily above. He was lost in his own thoughts, thoughts of how, as the leader of the alpha team, he could help his race. Help find those responsible for the attacks on his kind and satisfy the council all at the same time.

The council's attitude towards the recent abductions at the start had been encouraging, only now, they didn't seem to care very much. They were simply saving face, letting the innocent think they were doing all they could, when, in fact, they were doing nothing. It was the enforcers who were doing the work. It had always been that way, only now it seemed to grate on Dominic more.

Lately, the overall attitude of the council towards not only him but a few others had brought his own loyalty into question. Michael, the self-proclaimed leader of the council, had made it clear what he thought of Dominic on more than one occasion. He was considered a lesser being, one that should never have been given a position of high standing.

Dominic was a half-breed succubi. What his other half was, he had no idea. That had been a secret his dear mama had taken with her to her grave. Her reluctance to tell him—or anyone, for that matter—who and what his father was, had become a subject Dominic liked to avoid. He had spent the majority of his life being snubbed by those who thought themselves better than him due to their bloodlines. Pure bloods, exactly like Michael, had tried their best to bury Dominic beneath a heavy weight of discrimination. It would have worked—if Dominic had cared.

He didn't. Bloodlines meant nothing to him. For Dominic, he didn't care if you were green, blue, or had horns. Your actions spoke for you, not your blood. In short, an arsehole was simply that: an arsehole. It didn't matter if they were born royal or born poor.

Dominic had fought his way to his position with hard work and determination—and a touch of help from his brothers. Especially Sebastian.

The male had seen a young warrior with no clue how to control his body's changes and took him under his wings. Without Sebastian, Dominic would have never known how to channel his abilities, or stop them from draining him of energy. Dominic had extra abilities, ones he credited to his unknown half. At the start of his training, they had scared the living shit out of him. Sebastian had helped him find his feet as an enforcer, and then like a dutiful parent, he left him to the rest on his own.

He was the warrior he was today because of Sebastian, and for that, he would lay down his life for his brother. They had trained together, both flying up the ranks. Sebastian had been first in line for the leader of the enforcers; with his experience and skill, he was the perfect choice. Only, he had turned it down instead, stating that Dominic was born the leader and would make a far superior one. That had humbled him, as a half-breed to get to his position was an accomplishment. Michael had not liked it. As a purist, the mere thought of a half-breed now being in control of what was the succubi army made his left eye twitch.

It was that day that Michael had informed him, in hushed tones, that as a half-breed, he may run the enforcers, but he would never be chosen to bond with their females. He would never feel the joy of matehood or parenthood. The evil glint in the councilman's eyes had confirmed Dominic's gut reaction to the male.

Dominic had remained cool and calm, not letting the male or his words bother him. As far as that slimy fuck was concerned, Dominic had a heart of stone and only cared about his next mission. In a way, that was true; he focused on each mission, making sure his men knew their roles, and that if shit hit the fan, they would get out.

Dominic did not want dead males on his watch—ever.

His job was simple: protect the innocent and protect his race—even if most snubbed him. If he was burning alive, he wouldn't be surprised if they pulled out the marshmallows. His life as an enforcer also meant one thing: his life was forfeit; his race came first, and his men. That's what his life was. But when his end came, Dominic would make sure he went out like a true warrior.

Dominic shook his head, dispelling the heavy, depressing thoughts. He had no idea why they had turn so negative all of a sudden. He had become used to Michael's way with words and used to the bullshit he sprouted on a regular basis, so it confused him why, all of a sudden, he was drowning his sorrows due to that prick.

"Dom?"

Dominic placed the untouched glass of vodka back onto the table before his lifted his eyes slowly to meet those of his second in command.

"I thought I would find you here—even if I did say to avoid this place."

Sebastian turned the chair around in front of him and

straddled the wood, placing his arms on the back. The warrior, to him, looked far too casual compared to his usual demeanour. Sebastian was old school, so his act now made Dominic pause.

He didn't answer straight away. Instead, he picked his glass back up and knocked the liquid back in one go. The alcohol burned its way down his throat, and Dominic relished the slight buzz it gave him. Even if it did last for only a second, his metabolism burning though the alcohol quickly.

"Dom... I'm—" he started, then shook his head. Sebastian frowned and then started again. "The team are worried about you," Sebastian stated simply. He never did sugar coat anything.

"I'm fine, Seb—nothing a night of alcohol and a good fight won't fix." He smiled, but it was a false one. His team had picked up on his restlessness quickly.

For the past few weeks, he had been constantly on edge. Nothing could settle him, and he had felt more and more aggressive. Initially, he had put it down to the shock of seeing what humans had done to one of their own. Callum's female had been brutally tortured. But even now, when even Helena was making a good recovery, he couldn't use that as an excuse.

"Really? You're fine, are you?" Sebastian questioned, the sarcasm in his voice clear as crystal. "Ever since we got back from fetching Helena, you've been moody and have seemed to take the abductions to heart and the hunting of the ones responsible as your only mission. It's not all on you, Dom... As enforcers, it's on all of us."

Dominic lifted his eyes once again to those of his friend, who smirked back at him. "And the fact you have been a snappy bastard of late... Care to share?"

"Finished?" Dominic asked, trying his best to not snap. He knew his friend meant well, but it rubbed him the wrong way to know that he was so transparent.

"Not really." Sebastian shrugged. "We need you and the alpha team strong. We need to act as a unit and not have you fucking off on your own thinking you can take them all on. It will get you killed." Sebastian leaned forward and pinned Dominic with a hard look.

"Is that what you want Dom.... Death?"

Dominic didn't answer; he couldn't. The words wouldn't form in his throat. He should have known Sebastian would pick up on the changes he had fought so hard to hide.

Clever bastard.

No one knew those needs he had trained too hard to control had increased. His body was controlling him now with the need to feed almost every night riding him hard. An aggression he had never experienced before meant he was on the edge constantly. Ready to rip into anyone and anything. That's why he had kept a distance from his men. They didn't deserve him going rogue on them, and he was fully aware of the damage he was capable of.

Everything had increased; his strength, the amount of food he consumed. His clothes felt tighter and he had no idea why. The only answer was his unknown side was becoming dominant, and Dominic couldn't do anything to stop it.

For a succubi male, drinking blood was the norm, but only from their bonded mates. Dominic didn't have a bonded, but the need to drink was overwhelming. And the gift of a mate would never be his. Unclenching his fist from under the table, he looked at his large palms. No marks would ever grace them.

"Are you listening to me, Dom? We need to figure out what the hell is going on with you."

Dominic just shook his head. "Leave it."

"Fuck off will—" Sebastian stopped mid-sentence, his posture changing from relaxed to fully alert in seconds. Dominic frowned, until a moment later the smell hit him. His own body became taught, muscles flexed, readying themselves for a fight.

"Vampyre," he hissed. "What the fuck are they doing here?" Dominic turned his head slowly towards the bar. At the end, stood three males. All were the average height for a vamp—at six feet plus, they stood out compared to humans. All were dressed casually, but that didn't hide the fact they were predators, and there was only one reason they ventured into human bars:

They wanted to feed.

Engrossed in their own little bubble, the vamps had failed to notice the two warriors. That gave them an advantage—until Dominic noticed who they had focused on. He inhaled sharply as he watched the female who had haunted his dreams walk in. He had watched her like a stalker every time she had come into the bar. Dressed in tight black jeans that made his fingers twitch, the material clung to her curves like a second skin and made Dominic salivate.

Her hair, pulled into two French braids, sent his imagination into overdrive and all the blood in his system to pool south of the border. She was sin and sex encased in tight denim.

"Dom?" Sebastian moved to his side. "We can't take them here—too many humans," Sebastian advised, and tugged Dominic's arm, not realising Dominic didn't give a shit about the vamps anymore. His focus was on the female, and her alone. That voice in the back of his head was screaming to go to her. To touch her skin to see if it was as soft as it looked.

A snarl ripped from his throat as Sebastian turned him forcibly so he couldn't see the female anymore.

"Fuck, you are on edge, man. Come on outside. Now." Dominic knew Sebastian was right and allowed himself to be escorted outside. Though every step away from the female hurt, like needles digging into his skin.

Once outside, he forced air into his lungs. Deep breaths sawed in and out until he felt almost level-headed again.

"Dom—fuck, your eyes..." Dominic heard the panic in his friend's voice and closed his eyes, trying to calm himself. Recently, Dom's eyes had started to change from their usual bright green to a deep crimson.

"I've never seen you react to vamps like that, brother," Sebastian stated.

Dominic shook his head from his bent over position, hands on his knees. "It's not the vamps. That female..." He didn't complete the sentence as waves of pain flowed over his skin. "Fuck," he growled.

"That female?" Sebastian questioned. "She's just human, Dom." His friend was frowning down at him, concern in his eyes.

"I don't know, Seb. Fuck... I have no idea what's happening to me, but I know we can't leave her alone with those vamps. I'm fighting the urge to rip them apart for looking at her," Dominic admitted, and watched as his friend's eyes widened before he nodded and walked back to the door.

Dominic knew taking on three large vampyres was not a good idea, but he couldn't deny what his body was screaming at him. Leaning back against the wall, Dominic finally managed to calm a little, the idea that Sebastian had fetched the female making a good job of calming him down.

Wiping his hand across his mouth, he winced. Small cuts had split the flesh from where a set of fangs had erupted.

"That's new," he admitted.

The sound of the door opening had Dominic turning his head to see his friend walk out, worry across his face.

"Well? Where is she?"

"She's gone. The barman said she walked in, took one sip of her drink, and then left. Quickly."

"Right," Dominic replied, feeling disappointed.

"But..."

"But what," Dominic snapped, and stood up from the wall.

"The vamps have gone too. They followed her out."

The snarl that erupted from Dominic's mouth echoed off the walls of the back alley and had Sebastian stepping back. The look of surprise on his friend's face didn't really register as one word repeated in his skull:

Mine.

Cracking his neck, he moved towards the exit of the alley.

"Dom, where the hell are you going?" Sebastian reached out to grab Dominic's arm, only to back away when he snarled.

"Hunting," was the only answer he was able to give, the fangs that had erupted before peeking out from his top lip. Moving quickly into the street, he snarled again. That one word forcing his pace to increase and giving a voice to the word.

"*Mine.*"

5

Higher than a Vamp

THE PUNGENT SMELL OF CIGARETTES AND ALCOHOL HIT Constance's nose the moment she opened the door to Pulse. It definitely wasn't your normal London club. In fact, most would class it as a dive. Although smoking in pubs, clubs and restaurants had been banned, this place still allowed it. From the looks of things, the owners did what they wanted and were not bothered about being inspected. Again, unlike most places in the capital, it didn't have the usual queues of partygoers outside, and she preferred that. Constance hated crowds. Too many people set her on edge.

She smiled as she walked past the two bouncers, who instead of being outside, were enjoying a crafty pint themselves. Constance headed for her usual perch, at the end of the bar.

"Evening, sweetheart. Back again?" the deep voice of the barman called out. "The usual?" he added. She had never bothered to ask his name, just like he had never asked for hers, and she liked that. No one in here bothered you or asked questions. She smiled brightly as she slid onto the stool.

"Yes, please."

This had become Constance's routine. She would sit in her corner, and watch the comings and goings. She would also be checking for anyone who seemed suitable for her purpose. On her better days, Constance could almost feel like a femme fatale from the movies. Looking for her prey.

Smirking to herself, she shook her head. One of the other bonuses to her little perch was the view. Her skin prickled with awareness, and she didn't even need to turn around to know he was there. The hairs on the back of her neck lifted, as if reacting to his presence even from the other side of the room.

Constance smiled her thanks as the barman slid the small glass across the bar towards her. The dark liquid glimmered in the lights as she swirled it, and in one fluid motion, she knocked it back. On her short walk over to the bar, she had made a decision. A big one.

No longer would that man be the subject of her dreams and fantasies. No, instead she would get up off the stool and walk over to him. She turned her head to look at his profile, her eyes caressing his form. His relaxed posture made him more approachable, and the leather of his jacket pulled tight across his broad shoulders. Everything about this man created a response in Constance's body.

Sliding from the stool, she stood, ready to walk over— only to stop when another man sat down opposite him. The other man was equally as gorgeous, but he didn't fire her blood the way the first one did. His own face did not look impressed. In fact, he looked angry. Turning her back, she looked back at the bar. All the courage she had mustered to approach her fantasy man had now gone.

Her heart rate increased, and the hairs on the back of her neck once again rose. But it wasn't due to the man. No, this time it felt like a warning. One Constance wouldn't ignore. Something felt wrong, but she couldn't quite put her finger on it. Constance was ready to head for the door when a voice called out.

"Hey, princess." Constance made the mistake of turning her head to look at the owner of the voice. To her left were three men, all handsome in their own way. In the past, they would have been her go to type, but now, all they did was set off alarm bells in her head. Instead of responding, Constance turned and headed for the exit, eager to be out in the fresh air and get home.

"Hey, sugar, don't go yet," one of the men called out, but Constance was already pushing through the door. She was eager to get away and get back home.

Constance jammed her hands into the small pockets of her leather jacket and moved down the street. Her head bowed, she avoided eye contact with the many clubbers moving the other way. The hair on the back of her neck shot up, sending an answering shiver down her spine moments before another voice called out.

"Hey, we were talking to you!" Peeking over her shoulder, Constance saw it was the same three guys who had tried to strike up a conversation in the bar. Turning her head, she carried on walking, not wanting to make a scene or encourage them. Hopefully they would just give up and go and annoy someone else. It wasn't as if there weren't plenty of other women around to tempt them.

Mere seconds after that thought had crossed her mind, Constance felt arms around her waist and her body being lifted off the floor. A sweaty, large hand moved over her mouth, masking her shouts.

"Now we have your attention," the deep voice whispered into her ear. Constance struggled, trying her best to wriggle free from the vicelike grip he had on her. He briefly relaxed it, letting her feet drop to the floor, giving her time to bite down on his palm and slam her booted heel into his instep.

For a mere second, Constance felt a glimmer of hope that it would work, until he once again tightened his arms around her. Pinning his own arms to her side. He was so close she could smell his putrid breath as it whispered over the skin of her neck.

Lifting her eyes, she saw the other two men. One had his back to them. They had brought her into a dark alley, and this man was standing watch. The other, though, watched her, eagerness written across his face.

Constance felt the panic well up inside of her. Fear took over and she started to struggle again, kicking her legs and catching the men in the shins. Her captor's chuckle did nothing but scare her more, but it turned to a hiss as she caught him again. Slowly, he turned their bodies so she now faced the wall. The movement felt like slow motion as she felt a hand go into her hair and her face rammed into the brickwork.

"Fucking bitch!" he shouted.

Constance saw stars, felt the dull scrape of stone on her skin and her nose buckle under the pressure. Pain exploded through her, and her mind became a fog of regrets.

"Now, behave," the male sneered against her neck, moments before she felt the scrape of teeth against her skin. Only these teeth weren't dull. That thought flew from her mind as said teeth bit down, forcing a scream of pain from her. Her mind fractured and became a tangled mess of images; green eyes, the attack... and pain.

"Man... Hurry up, I want some." Her fogged brain picked up on the other male, who seemed closer than before.

The male who held her ground his obvious arousal into her arse as he drank her blood. She could feel each pull on her carotid, and with each pull, her life was syphoned away.

On the verge of unconsciousness, Constance felt the male withdraw, but also felt her body dropping to the ground. Her limbs wouldn't work to support her, so she free fell, and her head hit the concrete. Constance felt her body shudder as the cold settled into her body.

"Fuck..." the male murmured. "Her blood... fuck!"

His voice seemed slurred, and she watched as he stumbled. When he turned to look at her, he grinned in an almost goofy way. The way someone very high would do after a particularly good hit.

"Man, does she taste that good?" the other asked, stepping closer, the eagerness clear on his face. Constance watched as fangs slowly emerged and pressed into his lower lip. Her head must have hit the floor harder than she realised. Those couldn't be fangs.

Her vision wavered as the second man approached and bent down. None too gently, he grasped the braids of her hair and lifted her head off the floor.

"Is she really as good as you say?" he questions, turning to look up at his friends.

"Oh, that *and* some. Succubi," he stated as he leaned against the wall, enjoying his buzz.

"Mmm, really? I've always wanted some of that." His voice slid over Constance's nerves. She pulled what little strength she had left together and lashed out, using her nails to rake down the man's face. He dropped her head and hissed.

"Bitch! You should be enjoying this. You should feel honoured."

"Fuck you," Constance grated out as her head spun. She again felt fingers on her head, before he copied his friend's actions, slamming her face into the concrete.

"Quiet!" he shouted, before he pulled her neck up towards his mouth, her body now limp. A small part of her brain marvelled at his apparent strength. She felt his tongue slide across her skin, felt the rumble of enjoyment in his chest before pain once again detonated through her, quickly followed by her answering scream. Constance didn't fight the darkness encroaching on her vision.

Instead, she embraced it, wanting to fall into its dark and pain-free embrace.

Dominic's booted feet pounded against the pavement as he left the alley at the back of the bar. Already, he was at a disadvantage by being on the other side of the building to the entrance. He moved quickly.

Stealth wouldn't work. Instead, he needed speed and lots of it.

He tried to ignore the possessive thoughts that had started to repeat in his head for a female he didn't know—a human one at that. But as an enforcer, regardless of what race she belonged to, there was no way he could leave her to the mercies of bastard bloodsuckers who had no respect for themselves, never mind a female.

If he delved within his own feelings, it went a lot deeper than even he wanted to admit. The female had stirred emotions within him since the first day he had seen her. Emotions he needed to file away. But now, fear drove him; it pushed him forward—along with the knowledge there was a high probability he would have to fight to get to her. Adrenaline swept through his veins as his muscles bunched. His speed was inhuman but he didn't care who saw him. But being typical London, no one blinked an eye in response.

A scream rent the air, but no sooner had it filled the night, it cut off. Dominic felt his heart stop briefly. The scream's echo rebounded off the walls of the buildings surrounding them, making its location difficult to pinpoint. Until he caught her scent. It was there; a faint trail yet enough for him to zero in on a small alley.

The scents of the vampyre males filled the area. As he slowed to a walk, he studied the alley, and watched as a single male met him eye to eye before bolting down the road.

They were there, and now there were only two. The odds, though, were still stacked against them; the way Dominic was currently feeling, it would take more than three vampyres at full strength to beat him.

Dominic stalked into the alley, his hands free of any weapons. He wanted to be up close and personal as he delivered his blows, wanted them to see just how much he meant it. Something stirred within him at the prospect of delivering retribution with his bare hands.

The intense desire to hurt, maim, and kill rode him hard, especially when he found the female unconscious and being fed from. Dominic saw red, his vision narrowing down to the male feeding. Anger flowed through him, and he let it dictate his actions.

Not giving the vampyres any time to react, he lifted the one feeding from the female by the back of his neck and threw him against the far wall. The sound of crunching bone did nothing to settle the rage, so he turned on the other, who was leaning against the brick wall.

Dominic flew a glance behind him to make sure the female was there, and he was between her and the vamps.

At first glance, the second male seemed to be asleep, but on closer inspection, Dominic noticed the male was out of it. His swaying form and goofy grin seemed completely out of place. His rage diminished slightly, giving his mind the freedom to think logically. Stalking again to the second male, he reached out and wrapped his hand around his throat and squeezed. After only few seconds, the vampyre's eyes opened and his face slowly turned blue.

"What.... the ... fuck... man," the male choked out.

"Why her?" Dominic snarled. "There are plenty of women out tonight."

"Scent... taste... so... good..." the male again choked out. His eyes nearly bulged out of his skull, but Dominic could clearly see the effect the feeding had on the vampyre. Instead of the red ring that usually circled the iris when they fed, his was a burnished gold.

This male was high, but not only that... He was high from drinking from a succubi female.

6

Green-eyed Rescuer

"You knew she was succubi," Dominic growled out as he slammed the male's head into the bricks behind him.

"You knew what she was and yet you hunted her anyway," he snarled. Dominic released the male and watched as he bent over, trying to catch his breath. As soon as the male looked up, Dominic's fist shot out, throat punching the vampyre into unconsciousness.

"Son of a bitch," Dominic grated out, before he turned and quickly returned to the side of the female. Concern for her had him reaching out, checking for a pulse. He sighed in relief as he felt it, shallow but still there.

Her face was something he had come to dream about on many occasions, yet now, she was almost unrecognisable. Bruising covered her entire right side, and her nose was clearly broken. Blood seeped from wounds to her forehead and lip, and she also had a steady stream leaking from the jagged puncture wounds in her neck.

Rage again tore through him at their blatant mistreatment of a female who should be protected.

"Fucking leeches," he snarled out again, trying his best to stop himself from standing up and ripping the two unconscious males apart. For what they had done, he should really, but he didn't want a full-scale brawl between the succubi and the vampyres to erupt when they were on such unsteady ground as it was. He also needed to get the female into protective custody. How she had survived in the human world was a surprise to Dominic, but it was a question that would have to be asked later.

Right now, her current health was key.

Tilting her head, Dominic selfishly revelled in the feel of her skin, his thumb gently caressing as he checked out the bruising to her chin before turning to the open wounds on her neck. When vampyres fed, they injected a small amount of anticoagulant into their victims to make feeding easier. If they wanted, they could close the wounds with their tongues. But most didn't, instead leaving them to slowly bleed out.

If Dominic did nothing, the female would suffer the same fate, and that was something he would not allow. She was now his charge, and he would protect her with his life.

Bending his head, Dominic drew in a deep breath, committing her scent to memory. The smell of her blood called to him, firing his own in response. Ignoring his own body's needs, he swept his tongue gently over the two small puncture wounds, using the healing abilities in his salvia to close them and stop the bleeding.

Her taste was exquisite and surprised him. But what surprised him even more was the moan that fell from her lips as he drew his tongue over the now closed wounds. A moan that shot straight to his groin. Dominic pulled back and looked at the woman now in his arms. Her face so serene and peaceful before, now only showed confusion as he was faced with the most beautiful blue eyes in existence.

Confusion knitted her brow and made the bruising look more severe. He had expected fear, yet there was none, and that surprised him the most. Her whispered words pulled him from his silent worship of her beauty. The slight rasp in her voice reminded him again what she had already been through, and she didn't need him ogling her like he was.

"Who are you?" her calmness changed, panic started fill her voice telling him she wasn't just scared, she was petrified.

"A friend. I'm here to help you," Dominic answered, and watched her carefully, looking for any signs that she was about to lose it. He wouldn't have blamed her at all—hell, if he'd had a run in with vampyres like she had, he would have lost his shit as well.

Gently bringing her body into his own, he cradled her within his arms. He felt her stiffen, and the panic that had been on the edge flared to life within her blue eyes.

She started to shake, her body fighting his hold as she bucked. Her hoarse voice cried out. "Get off me! *Get off me!*"

Dominic was lost at the sight of her tears as they fell freely from her eyes, and released his hold on her slightly. Hoping to show her in deed that he didn't mean her any harm.

"Shhh, it's ok," he cooed.

"Get off!" she screamed again, and he winced as the high-pitched sound hit his eardrums. "Get fucking off!" she cried out, and again, Dominic had no choice but to release his hold on her.

She wobbled as she stood, her eyes flying from him to

the downed males behind. Dominic stayed still, his arms out to the side.

"It's ok," he called out, and watched as her fear-filled eyes shot to his. It took seconds, but it felt like days, for her own blue orbs to widen as she recognised him.

"You," she breathed. "Did you...?" Her question blurted out as she looked again at the males on the floor.

"I stopped them," he answered.

"They bit me," she whispered as her hand went to her neck. She winced, before her eyes went wide, and Dominic fired himself forward before her body could hit the floor. Collecting her back into the safety of his arms, he felt her stiffen again.

"Shh, it's ok. I'm going to get you home," he stated calmly. "I promise, nothing will hurt you now," he spoke honestly. Nothing would hurt her, and he would personally make sure of it. That possessive feeling he had felt on leaving the bar returned, only this time he didn't ignore it. He used it to fuel his protective rage. While she was in his care, nothing and no one would hurt her.

He felt her settle in his arms, her right one lifting to wrap around his neck as her face settled into the crook of his shoulder. Contentment like nothing he had ever felt in his life, hit him. Holding her like this felt perfect. Dominic felt himself give her a gentle squeeze before he walked out of the alley. Looking both ways, he gauged the distance to the portal. Without the back up of his team, he didn't want to risk taking her there.

"Where do you live, sweetheart?" he asked calmly, his face only inches from her head. He couldn't stop himself from breathing in the sweet scent of her hair.

Slowly, she turned her head and looked up at him. Their faces only inches apart, Dominic was lost in her blue eyes.

"Archer Gardens," she started, although her voice was slightly slurred, and her lids repeatedly drooped, "Block C, flat 23."

Dominic nodded and smiled a little. He watched her place her head back onto his shoulder and close her eyes. Turning his head, Dominic looked back into the alley, happy to see the two vampyres were still out cold. Moving towards the right, Dominic set a quick pace. He knew Archer Gardens. It was on the edge of one of the seedier parts of London. A place a female, never mind a succubi one, should not be living.

Dominic wanted to get her home, get her packed, and then get her to the safety of Helvetia. There, she would be protected. She was a rare gift to his race, and a welcome one. She would be treated like a queen and be bonded with a strong male.

That thought churned through Dominic's gut. The idea of her with another male didn't sit right and made his left eye twitch.

She wasn't his to covet, and by the will of the council never would be.

But... she set something off inside of him, something he struggled to fight. A deep, dark part of his soul, a selfish part, screamed that she was his and his alone. Only he knew the truth. He wasn't worthy of a female like her.

As Dominic increased his pace down the road, her quiet voice pulled him from his inner turmoil. Its soothing tone eased the rage slightly.

"Thank you," she whispered, although her eyes remained shut. "What's your name?" she asked, and Dominic answered, somehow eager for her to know who he was.

"Dominic."

"Dominic," she repeated. The way she said his name slid over his nerves, calming him. No woman in his whole existence had ever been able to calm his rage. Not like she was able to do.

"You look like a Dominic," she whispered again, her lips tilted into a small smile when he looked down at her.

"And what does a Dominic look like?" The question burst from his lips. He wanted to keep her talking, keep her focused on him.

"Like you," she answered again. "Tall, strong, gorgeous... green eyes." Her words became quieter as she slowly gave up to unconsciousness. His eyes widened at her compliment, although he reckoned, fully awake, she would have never said it.

"Thank you, Dominic."

"You're welcome, sweetheart," he replied, and smiled.

"Constance," she murmured.

"What?" Dominic asked, only this time he stopped and looked down at the beauty in his arms.

"My name... Constance." Her reply was cut short as she finally gave in, her body needing the rest, and Dominic was glad. Her name repeated over and over in his head.

Shifting her higher in his arms, he started to walk again. His precious cargo would need the entire alpha team to get her back home to Helvetia. With that in mind, he quickened his pace.

"It's ok, Constance. I've got you."

7

Even Home isn't Safe

THE THIRD VAMPYRE WATCHED AS THE ENFORCER CARRIED THE female away from his friends. Any other male, and he would have made a move, but he wasn't stupid enough to go up against the notorious Umbra (shadow), leader of the enforcers and alpha team. Dominic was not a warrior to be messed with—even alone. His friends had been stupid, too eager to take a taste of the female instead of getting her back to one of the safe houses where they could have all had fun.

But now he had a problem. Their lord and master had demanded to know if a succubi female was ever found, and if so, she was to be taken straight to him. The male cracked his next and followed slowly, keeping downwind so the warrior wouldn't sense him.

Pulling out his mobile, he hit the speed dial, his eyes never leaving the form of the enforcer.

"What!" the deep voice answered.

"My lord, myself, Carl and Bart have located a female." He kept it simple. His master was not a man, or vampyre, of many words.

"Secure her," he ordered, and the male felt sweat beading on his brow.

"My lord, it is not that simple. Carl and Bart have already tasted her, and then they were set upon by an enforcer."

"Where is she now?" his master asked, his calm voice making the male shake.

"She is being taken somewhere by the enforcer male. He is alone. He did not kill Bart or Carl, either." The male rattled off as much information as he could, and waited.

"Listen," his master started, "you need to secure that female before that enforcer gets back up."

"But—but, my lord..." Fear shivered up the male's spine. To face off alone against an enforcer, especially Dominic, meant his death. He was not, and never claimed to be, a warrior. "It's no normal enforcer, It is The Umbra."

"I don't care who he is. You go and get her," his master's voice shouted down the line, the power he wielded snaking up his spine. The male's knees almost weakened.

"I want her. Get it done." With that, the line went dead, and so did the male's heart. He had no choice. Either take on the most lethal enforcer and die, or return to his master empty-handed and die.

He was dead either way.

8

Burdens—Precious Ones

DOMINIC MOVED QUICKLY, CAREFUL NOT TO JOSTLE THE precious burden within his arms. He knew of Archer Gardens, so it didn't take him long to get there, but he felt a frown marring his forehead when he approached what he hoped wasn't her building. The grounds were unkempt, with graffiti decorating the walls. Some doors were devoid of glass, and the street lights were nearly all broken.

The area gave off a *don't linger* vibe that had the hairs on the back of Dominic's neck rising. The only difference now was he was a damn sight scarier than any of the delinquents who thought they ruled this place.

His respect for Constance grew. She had managed to live here alone. How, he had no clue. What concerned him was the why. Did she not realise what she was? That had to be the only explanation for how a mature succubi female was alone in London. Only, that thought made him frown more. Surely, she would have turned without the presence of her bonded male, and there were clearly no marks on her hands to say she was bonded. That, and her scent was devoid of any males.

Constance was a conundrum, his very own puzzle box just waiting to be figured out. Ignoring the skulking shadows, Dominic moved until he stood outside the building named Block C. Luckily, this seemed to be the only building that had retained a locked door and intact glass, along with working lights. That still didn't put him at ease.

Tilting his head to look down at Constance, his eyes roamed over her face, taking in the full lips, petite nose, and long eyelashes. He even committed to memory the small scar over her left eyebrow. Its faint line glimmered slightly in the light.

"Constance," he murmured gently, and felt his chest expand slightly when she tried to burrow closer to him.

"Come on, beautiful, you need to wake up," he cajoled. He needed her to wake so he could get her into the building and into a secure area. Being out in the open made him twitch. He didn't know how many vampyres were aware of his charge, but he wouldn't put it past the bastards to try and retrieve her.

"Constance, we are home." Those words... What he wouldn't give to actually say them and have them ring true. This may be her home, but she didn't belong here. A sense of longing ripped through Dominic, and he fought it back. Feelings like that would only cause trouble, and he was already in enough of that with the way his body reacted to her.

Slowly, her blue eyes opened and looked up at him. They were still unfocused and drowsy due to the trauma she had been through. As a succubi female, she should heal quickly, but instead, the bruising remained the same and the cut to her forehead had scabbed at a human rate. She needed to feed from a member of her own race. That had to be the only explanation for how and why she hadn't turned. If she had never fed, then her body would have never gone through that phase.

Although there was still the fact her body gave off the scent of arousal, it was muted. Yet still there, like she was on the cusp. Dominic tightened his hands has he remembered her in the bar over the past few months. Every time, leaving with another male. Things slotted into place, and he fought back the growl that wanted to escape at the thought of her being intimate with all those males; letting them put their hands on her silky, soft skin, being able to hear her cry out in pleasure. They didn't deserve the honour—hell, even Dominic didn't, but it didn't stop him from wanting it.

She still didn't say anything, just looked up at him with eyes so wide he could have drowned in their depths. What was it about this female that threw his whole equilibrium sideways?

Dominic perched on a wall by the door to her block. Moving his hand, he was able to push a lock of hair away from her face, finally able to touch her soft skin again under the pretence that he was checking her injuries. The bruising was dark and clear, her pale skin, the dried blood still present, and Dominic wanted nothing more than to hunt the two responsible all over again.

"How are you feeling?" he asked. His fingers stilled against her temple.

"Groggy. Sore," she answered, her voice slightly husky, which caressed his nerves, soothing the constant anger that had been his friend lately. Gently, he sat her up in his lap— not too fast as he didn't want her fainting, but slowly enough for her to get her bearings. He expected her to move away from him, but instead, she kept her hands on his chest, almost like she needed to touch him as much as he needed to touch her. The affect she had on him was worrying.

"Thank you," she said again, and tried to smile but winced when the cut on her lip opened again. Their faces were close, close enough that Dominic could smell the toothpaste and alcohol mix. Close enough that the scent of her blood from the cut called to him. He watched as her own eyes widened, as they flicked to his own lips.

Her thoughts were there, plain as day, on her face; the need clear as crystal, and Dominic's own body agreed. He wanted to taste her lips, to plunge his tongue into the deep recesses of her mouth. He wanted to hear her moan with pleasure as he took his own, dominating the kiss like a true warrior should. He was close... a mere inch away, when the hitch in her breath and the widening of her eyes brought back focus.

Fear, clear as day, was etched onto her face, and Dominic, for a split second, was convinced it was him. Until the scent hit him.

Vampyre.

Turning his head, he watched the male stalk closer, fangs fully erupted. Dominic gently placed Constance on her feet and moved them so they were within the doorway. Turning her so she faced him instead of their new friend, he kept his eyes on the male but leaned down to whisper in her ear.

"Sweetheart, I need you to get inside. Can you do that?" He waited, his hands on her shoulders, his thumbs caressing them in a gentle manner. She nodded slowly, but her breathing was coming in gasps, signalling a panic attack.

"Good girl. Get inside and shut the door. Don't watch." Dominic didn't wait for a reply. Instead, he stepped around her so she was behind him, and faced the vampyre. Dominic moved his head from side to side, the sound of his bones cracking echoing in the night air.

His focus on the male in front, Dominic was pleased to hear the door open and then close as Constance did as he asked. Now he could play.

Dominic clenched his fists and slowly reached behind to draw his two favourite knives from the hidden sheaths. Spinning them in his hands, he gave the male a dark look.

"Time to play."

Constance watched from behind the glass door as Dominic turned and faced off with another man. At first glance, he seemed like a regular guy. That was until she took in the red eyes and lengthening fangs. She watched, in horror, as his hands went from normal to creepy in seconds. Claws—well, more like talons—erupted from his nail beds.

Surely that wasn't real. Maybe she had hit her head harder than she thought.

That thought vanished quickly, despite the fact she felt like she had been hit by a truck and her head had an entire brass band within it, firing off the full version of *Land of Hope and Glory*. She stood, wide-eyed. Her hands gripped the door handle.

There was no way Dominic could take this guy. He looked like an extra from a vampire movie, and then some. Her thoughts soon changed as they charged each other, like a class of gladiators. From somewhere, Dominic had grabbed knives and was using them like they were an extension of himself. His movements fluid-like and holding a grace a man of his size shouldn't possess.

Watching his body move mesmerised Constance. Sure,

she had seen men fight—she saw an awful lot of that in clubs these days—but this was something different. Her initial reaction to whether she thought Dominic could win was blown away.

He was a whirl of fists and knives, and his attacker knew it. She could see the defeat already in the depths of his eyes when they briefly lifted to meet her own. The thought of someone being killed right in front of her should be sending her into a full-blown panic, but instead, she watched in awe, waiting for her rescuer to deliver the final blow.

Dominic stalked his prey, and she watched every single movement, entranced. He kept his back to her at all times, even when the other tried to get past. In a move that surprised her, she watched as Dominic fell to one knee.

She gasped. No, he couldn't be defeated.

Her heart pounded against her chest as the other male, his fangs now dripping with blood and saliva, stalked closer. His arm and claws raised high, ready to take Dominic out. Victory at his grasp.

Pounding on the glass, Constance cried out, "No!"

The man smirked up at her as he stood over Dominic, as if to make sure she was watching when he struck. How had her rescuer gone from winning to losing? Without any thought for herself or the pain she was in, she pushed open the door.

"Oi, ugly," she called out, and was rewarded as a hiss filled the air and blood-red eyes focused solely on her. But she had to do something to stop him hurting Dominic. Shaking off the new feelings towards her rescuer, Constance eyed the attacker. Her body shook from not only earlier events, but fear.

She wasn't ashamed to say the sight scared her—so did

the thought of having those dang fangs rip her throat out—but she stood her ground.

"You really should get those teeth checked," she taunted. "I'm sure a few fillings would sort the issue out." Where the strength in her voice had come from she didn't know, but she kept her eyes focused on the man and hoped Dominic was ok.

He had to be.

The attacker, as planned, ignored Dominic and slowly stalked towards her, making her back up a step. Shit, this was not good.

"My master will be pleased with you. But first, I want a taste, female," he hissed, his body now only a foot or so away. Sweat beaded on her brow, and she could feel it as it dripped between her breasts.

This was not good. The smell of his rancid breath reached her, and she gagged. The idea of this man getting his hands on her made her step back again, until she was plastered against the glass of the door.

Time slowed as she watched his clawed hand reached out, his talons close to her throat as his eyes flared with hunger. Constance froze. Closing her eyes, she waited for the killing blow. Waited to feel the pain as he feasted on her flesh, just like she had seen in those horror films.

Only, nothing happened. Instead, she heard a loud thud, before she felt a presence. Only this time, it didn't feel threatening. Peeking one eye open, she looked into an angry set of green eyes.

"What the fuck did you think you were doing?" Dominic's voice shouted at her, causing her to wince as her headache went from subdued back to full on orchestra.

Her eyes flicked from his to the now fallen attacker, before Dominic moved in the way, blocking her view.

"Is he...?"

"Dead? Yes—unless the vamps found a way to grow back body parts," he stated, his voice calmer but his eyes still holding a trace of rage.

"What the hell were you thinking?" he asked again, stepping closer to her so she was still pressed against the glass.

"You were down," she answered. "I was—" she started but wasn't allowed to finish. She thought she saw a softening in his eyes, but it was gone in a flash.

"You could have been hurt. Never, and I mean never, do anything so reckless again," he growled out, getting well within her personal space.

Constance felt a mixture of emotions as she faced down with the man in front of her. A large part of her wanted to climb him like a pole and see if his lips felt as soft as they looked, but another part wanted to cause some sort of damage. She had saved him, dammit.

"I saved you," she blurted out, only to be met by a smug grin. And didn't that just rub her up the wrong way.

"Trust me, sweetheart, I wasn't in any danger." He finally stepped back and folded his big, beefy arms across his chest.

Jesus, how big are his biceps, a part of her brain piped up. Pushing the perv inside her head to one side, she glared at Dominic. She hated being laughed at.

"You know what? Up yours," Constance snapped, and turned her back on Dominic. She grabbed the door handle and pulled, but nothing happened. Tugging again, she growled in frustration.

"Need a hand?" His voice caressed her nerves as he moved behind her, and didn't that just make her girly bits wake up. She'd always had a thing for when a guy moved behind her, caressing her neck and wrapping her in his strength. But it hadn't really happened. Dominic wasn't even touching her, yet she could feel his heat, could almost feel his breath on her hair.

"I got this," she answered again, the heat in her voice almost gone as a husky edge replaced it.

"Sure?" he asked again. She swore he felt closer.

Constance turned and was eye level with a large chest. "I said..." Her sentence didn't finish as a wave of dizziness hit her, buckling her knees and almost sending her to the floor.

"Fuck," she managed to grate out, before she was happily once again in Dominic's arms.

"Constance?" he asked, his voice now filled with worry.

"Dizzy," she answered, and he snorted.

"Yeah, I guessed that. Come on, let's get you inside. What number you at, sweetheart?"

"Thirty-two," she answered as he moved her to one arm so he could open the door.

"Oh my god!" Constance gasped as she got to see the now decomposing corpse of her attacker, his body disintegrating in front of her.

"God?" He snorted as he moved her into the foyer and towards the stairs. "He doesn't concern himself with the lives of demons, sweetheart."

Not answering, she instead kept her eyes on his chest, tracing the fine detail on the material of his jacket so she wouldn't think about the sightless eyes staring up at her from the head of the attacker. A head that was two feet away from his body and crumbling to dust.

This had nothing on any horror film she had seen. How had her life gone from shite to totally fucked up in the space of a few hours?

9

Loyalty of the Alphas

SEBASTIAN MOVED OUT OF THE ALLEY AND SLOWLY FOLLOWED his friend. He didn't need to rush. There was simply no need. Whatever Dominic was going through, he needed an outlet for the rage he had seen burning in his friend's eyes.

A sure-fire way to clear it was to have a little rumble with the local bloodsuckers. Hell, Sebastian could do with that himself. The recent issue with immortals going missing had him on edge. He was grateful they had found the female, Helena. It meant their team would no longer be down a man. Callum was an asset to the Alphas.

The Alphas had always been a close-knit unit, but lately they seemed to be coming apart at the seams. Dominic was their leader, and they would give their lives for him, but lately, he was a loose cannon, and they were simply waiting for the explosion.

Sebastian had known his leader from an early age. He

had been there to see the hurt and pain caused when he was left with no one. Dominic was a force to be reckoned with, always had been, and it was why Sebastian had stepped down from being the one in charge. Dominic was born to lead.

He would support his friend, protect him even if he did so from himself. The female had to be the cause, as the issues had only started when Dominic had first seen her. Sebastian had known she would be trouble. Seeing Dominic in near rage, going after her and the vampyres, only confirmed it. Whatever spell she had over his friend, he would break it.

Walking down the road, Sebastian's senses searched for any sign of Dominic, only to come up short near an alley. The stench of vampyre and succubi blood had him breaking into a run. As he rounded the corner, he saw two vamps sprawled on the floor, their faces relaxed in a euphoric state. Their bruised throats and faces told him Dominic had indeed been here.

Moving closer, the vampyres took no notice of him. Instead, they smiled to themselves, enjoying the high. A high that could only come from limited sources, and as there were no stoners or crack heads about, and only the smell of succubi blood, he had an idea.

Turned out the little female wasn't the simple human they had mistaken her for, and it also answered the question, in part, about why his friend reacted to her. One of the reasons succubi females were protected was in large part to the blood they carried. To their own kind, the males, it was a life source and a way to bond mates.

To vampyres, it was likened to marijuana, only times ten and coupled with an aphrodisiac. It was highly sought after, and the vamps did whatever they could to get it. When a vampyre fed from a succubi female, she would then, in turn, become addicted to his bite.

Sebastian sighed. His own hurt and memories of his past tried to push to the forefront of his mind. He pushed back, sealing them deep inside.

After the vampyres were tired of the females, they would be released, but they were changed. Unable to feed from males of their own race, they suffered, mentally breaking down with addiction to a vampyre's bite. Most turned and had to be put down.

At one point, the vampyres had managed to wipe out near on a quarter of their race's females, all because of their selfish stupidity.

"I fucking hate vampyres," Sebastian growled, and moved away from the males on the floor. He wanted to snap their necks, but he wouldn't waste his breath and energy. These males were no threat, not now. Instead, he walked out of the alley and pulled his phone from his back pocket.

He needed Dominic's location, because if he was now guarding a female, he would need back up. Pinging a text to the team and to Dominic, he started a swift walk down the road he knew his friend had gone. The faint scent of the female still lingered in the air.

His earlier assessment of the female changed. He would, as would his brothers, protect her with his life. There was nothing more precious to his race than a female.

10

Handsome yet Irksome

CONSTANCE DIDN'T SPEAK AS DOMINIC CARRIED HER UP THE stairs. She didn't think she could actually form any sort of coherent sentences. What she had seen shouldn't be real. But she *had* seen it, and as much as she wanted this to be a dream, it wasn't. Which meant the fangs in her neck, back in the alley, were real, and that was something she didn't think she could process.

Dominic's booted steps echoed in the corridor as he moved steadily to her front door. The plain black wood came into view and Constance relaxed a little. This was home, her sanctuary. Constance tipped her face up to look at the man who had not only featured in every one of her fantasies, but had also saved her life not once, but twice. His profile was strong, and being this close, she could see details she hadn't seen before. Like the small scar on his chin, and the fact his nose had a slight bump to it. Or the fact his green eyes darkened when he looked at her like he was doing now.

Constance could do one of two things as his gaze intensi-
fied. She could either turn away, pretending she wasn't
checking him out, or she could just keep right on staring.
Constance had never been one to back down, so she kept up
her perusal.

Without blinking, Dominic spoke. His deep voice had an
edge to it Constance had never heard before, and it sent a
shiver up her spine. "Thirty-two?"

"What?" she asked, distracted by the heat she had seen
in his gaze, the green turning to emerald.

"Your door number," he stated again, and Constance
struggled to get her brain to work.

"Err... yeah."

"I'm going to put you down now. You tell me if you're
feeling dizzy still, ok?" She nodded in response—although
the perv in her head wanted to pretend she still felt dizzy,
just so she could stay in his arms. Slowly, she felt him
release her legs as he let her get her bearings, but he didn't
release his hold on her. The feel of his big hands cupping
her waist sent tingles shooting through her.

"Thank you," she answered, sneaking a peek to his face
again, and was rewarded with a slight smile and a nod.
Turning, she fumbled for her keys. Her hands shook with a
mind of their own, and she cursed in frustration.

"Let me." Dominic's voice whispered in her ear as he
reached over and plucked the keys from her grasp, before
making quick work of getting inside her flat. Before she was
able to take a step inside, he moved in front, his body
blocking hers he stalked inside.

"Hey!" she called out, only to have a hand held up for
her to be quiet. She felt her anger rising again. Stomping
past Dominic into her flat, she growled.

"No one's in my bloody flat, alright, Rambo. Stand

down." Ignoring his growl, she removed her jacket and threw it onto the sofa, before she moved into her bedroom just off the corridor and through to the small bathroom. She shut the door and locked it, then sat on the toilet seat and placed her head in her hands.

Flashes of what had happened filtered through her mind. She should be dead.

Standing, Constance looked at her reflection in the mirror. Her braids were a mess, and chunks of hair had come loose. The side of her face was a combination of colours, purple and black being the most defined. The cut in her hairline no longer oozed, and neither did the puncture wounds at her neck. She didn't doubt her whole body was covered with bruises now, but she didn't have the energy to deal with that at the moment.

Running the water, she grabbed a cloth and made quick work of cleaning her face and neck. Her tank top was ruined, so she quickly pulled it off, leaving her standing in her black jeans and a bra. Taking her time, Constance undid the two braids until her hair fell loose around her shoulders. She tired finger combing it, but it was too tangled. Feeling a tad bit more human, she unlocked the door and walked into her bedroom.

What she hadn't expected was for Dominic to be stood right by the door, his big body relaxed as he leaned against the wall. Only his eyes moved, watching her like a cat would a mouse. Constance stopped for a second, before she tried to ignore him and moved towards her chest of drawers. Quickly, she pulled out another tank top and slipped it over her head. She slowly pulled her long hair out of the top and reached for a hairbrush. Parking her butt on the bed, she looked up at the man who had rescued her.

"So... you going to tell me what the hell is going on?" she

asked. She still felt like shit, but she needed to know all the information. It was how she dealt with crap. She could then decide on a course of action.

Dominic didn't move. How many times had she imagined him in her room? Only, in her head, he had been naked and doing something a damn sight more interesting than being a part of her furniture.

"What you were attacked by and saw out front was a vampyre."

"A vampire?" she asked.

"No. A vampyre. There is a difference." This time he did move. In two steps, he reached the bed, and she watched as his big body gently sat.

Jesus! He was on her bed.

Constance's heartrate picked up. Her body, now free of fear, felt the return of her other issue. Need would course through her. It always did.

"I am..." he started, "a warrior."

"I guessed that." Constance snorted, but then pressed her lips together as his green eyes pinned her with a stare.

"Just saying," she blurted out again.

"I am a protector for my race, along with others. We are called Enforcers and we protect the innocent."

"What race?" Constance asked, leaning forward, the move not missed by the man in front of her

"You've heard of demons, right?"

Constance nodded but didn't say anything.

"Centuries ago, demons had free rein on Earth. We didn't hide in the shadows. But then came a war. Humans versus the immortals. It started with the witch trials. No one was safe. So, to try and maintain peace, many races withdrew to another realm. One we call Helvetia."

Constance frowned. "So why are you here?"

"Helvetia is the place we can retreat to, but we still deal with humans—do business with them as well," he stated simply.

"Demons..." she asked. "What kind of demons?"

"I'm a succubi, Constance," he answered. And didn't her body just melt at the way he said her name.

"Sex demon..." She frowned again.

"Not far wrong, but again, the humans' myths and legends have been distorted throughout the ages."

"Ahh. Err... ok," she answered.

"So, you're not like them? Like that thing outside?" she asked, nervousness in her voice

"No, Constance, I'm not," he sighed. "I'm sorry you had to see me fight, but he needed to be stopped."

"I'm not sorry, Dominic. Thank you for protecting me," she breathed out, forgoing the fact that watching him fight had been sexy and, thinking back, a turn on as well.

"Why did those men come after me?" she finally asked. "I'm nothing special."

"Now, in that, you are wrong, Constance." His eyes met hers and the green darkened further. In answer, her pulse sped up again. If she didn't watch it, she would have a heart attack with the amount of ups and downs her pulse was doing.

"I'm human. Definitely nothing special there." She stood and walked across the room. She was human. There was no way she was a... demon. Like him. Unless...

"Oh my god, he bit me. I'm going to turn. Oh my god!" Constance put her hand to her mouth. She was so screwed.

"Shhhhh." Dominic's voice came up behind her, and his hands caressed her shoulders. "You will not turn, Constance. It takes more than one bite to turn into a vampyre, and besides, you can't be turned, anyway."

"Why?" she turned and whispered up to him.

"Because of what you are." His thumbs played over the skin of her shoulders, making it difficult for her to think.

"What am I?"

Dominic hated seeing the fear within Constance's eyes, but she had to know the truth. She had to know that she wasn't human but something far more precious.

"You are succubi, like me, Constance," he stated simply. He could see her mind going over the information he had already given her. Only her head shook in denial.

"No, I can't be." She shook her head again. "I'm human."

"Sweetheart, you are far from human."

"Yes, I am. I just—"

"Just what?" he asked.

"Nothing," she answered, and turned away from him. She needed to understand that her life would be different now, and he needed to get her back to Helvetia.

"Constance, when was the last time you came?" He knew it was a low blow, using the issue he knew she had against her, but he didn't have much time.

"How dare you!" She spun and faced him, the rage he had known she hid coming to the forefront. And didn't she look magnificent. Her long hair caressed her shoulders and made him jealous. Since when had he been fucking jealous of hair? He wanted to dive his hand into the locks and pull her towards him, but he held back. Instead, she got into his face.

"That is none of your fucking business, regardless of the fact you saved my life."

"Twice."

"What?"

"Sweetheart, I saved your life twice and don't forget it. Now I know full well you haven't had an orgasm and that your body's needs is the reason I have seen you constantly in the bar and leaving with different men." He stalked forward, making her back up a step.

"You know nothing about me," she snapped, and turned her back on him.

He could see her shoulders as they heaved. Yes, she was angry with him, but she was also turned on—and didn't that just kick his own arousal up a notch. Not that it needed it. The fact they were near a bed had him clenching his fists in an effort to stop himself throwing her onto the mattress and giving her that elusive orgasm. Yes, he was that confident he could do it. He would make her cry out so loud with pleasure the entire neighbourhood would know his name.

Dominic fought back a groan.

And suddenly he couldn't help himself. He moved forward until he was behind her. Her sweet behind pressed against his groin as he leaned over her.

"I know you fight your body, Constance. Daily. I know nothing works—not even putting your own hand to your sweet pussy will relieve the ache. No man you have slept with," Dominic growled low at the thought, but continued, "could ever help you, instead leaving you worse off."

His breath whispered across her skin, and he drew in her scent, committing it to memory.

"How do you know this?" she whispered, turning her head so their mouths were mere inches apart.

"I know a lot of things, sweetheart." He smiled and moved his arms, wrapping them around her waist and bringing her into his body. This was wrong on so many levels, but he had fantasised about doing this since the first time he had seen her in the bar. It was his duty to protect her, not manhandle her, but her body called to his, silencing any protest in his mind.

"You want to know what can stop your body aching?" he began, as one hand stayed on her stomach, moving the material out of the way so he could touch bare skin, while the other moved up and swept her long hair back, giving him access to the graceful arch of her neck.

"Yes," she breathed, and he grinned, male pride filling him.

"Want to know what can help you get release, Constance?" he whispered, and she answered this time with only a nod. Her mouth was inches from his own as he pressed his hard length against her arse. He groaned when she pushed back eagerly.

"Me," he growled out, and his lips took hers in a bruising kiss. The moment he tasted her, Dominic knew, without a doubt, he would never get enough of her. He felt like one of those vamps eager for his next hit, because Constance was his drug. He swept his tongue into her mouth, dominating her and bending her to his will. Only she met him, her own tongue duelling with his and stirring him like no other.

Reluctantly breaking the kiss, he moved to her neck, pressing small kisses to the skin as she arched against him. She needed this. Hell, he needed this. Her body against his was heaven, a rightness that he didn't want to deny.

"Oh god," she gasped, her hand grabbing the one at her waist and moving it up until his hand cupped her breast. Her nipple peaked behind the material of the bra. Dominic squeezed gently, gaining another sultry moan.

With his other hand, he brushed her arm and tugged the strap of her tank top down, giving him more access to her skin. He wanted to taste her everywhere. Take his sweet time and learn every single spot that would give her pleasure.

Bringing his mouth to her shoulder, he sucked the skin before giving it a gentle bite. He couldn't help the grin as she moaned louder. Oh, his little Constance was a noisy one, and couldn't wait to hear her when she finally released. Dominic moved lower down, shifting the material of her top out of the way until something caught his eye. Moving back, his looked at the deep red mark that sat on her left shoulder. A frown marred his forehead as he tilted his head to look at it more. A sense he had seen it before washed over him.

"Dominic," Constance's voice called out, but still he stared, until recognition hit, and he hissed.

"Fuck!"

Pulling his hands from her body, Dominic stepped back as if he had been burned. His eyes only saw the mark, even when Constance turned to face him, her face a mask of need, her lips swollen from his kisses, and her top hoisted up from where his hands had sought her skin.

Her lust-filled eyes gazed at him, and Dominic fought his own body's needs. Fought the need to take her to the bed and make her his completely.

Only he didn't.

She had that mark, which meant he couldn't touch her. Hell, he shouldn't have touched her, period.

His eyes met hers again.

"Get packed. We are leaving here in ten," he snapped, and turned around, stalking out of the room and out of the flat, slamming the door as he went.

His body was still filled with the need to have her, but he couldn't. To do so would mean his own death.

She was forbidden to him.

11

———

Forbidden Fruit

"Fuck!" Dominic repeated as he slammed out of the door to Constance's flat. His body was so highly strung he was struggling to focus. Everything in him screamed to go back inside and finish what they had started. Since finding out she was a female of his race, he had felt his protective instincts surge forward, closely followed by lust. She was beautiful and her responses to his touch left him on the verge of losing himself like a young male. The brief hint at heaven was all it would be. Just a hint.

Now clear of her drugging scent, he could think a little clearer, but with that came the rage. Not at her but at himself. He had crossed a line he had sworn he never would. He had committed treason. It was that simple.

Booted feet echoed in the building, and Dominic raised his head as the first of the alpha team rounded the stairwell and approached him. When Constance had been in the bathroom, he had called for his team, only to find a text from Sebastian saying they were on their way and to confirm his location.

That was the only thing he was grateful for right now. His team were the best and the hardest. With them at his back to help escort Constance back to Helvetia, he knew no one would mess with them. He eyes watched his men as they entered the hallway, knowing that what he would reveal would not only change his life as an enforcer, but theirs too.

"Dom, nice to see you in one piece. Did you have much trouble?"

Dom tipped his head at each man in turn, and then answered Sebastian. "Only one male followed us. He was no threat."

"Yeah, we saw your welcome present, Dom. Nice work," Cooper called out from the back as he lit a cigarette.

Dom ignored him and instead looked at the other warriors. "Is the perimeter secure?"

"Yes," Alec answered. "Although the area leaves much to be desired."

"So... an unclaimed female?" Cooper called out, and Dominic growled. Cooper was a ladies man, but there was no way he would have Constance anywhere near him. His rage had returned, drowning out the lust.

"Cooper, once again, shut the fuck up," Sebastian snapped. "She wouldn't want your trashy arse anyway."

"I'm not trashy." He pouted.

"Whore," Alec called out, and smirked.

"Enough!" Dominic shouted, and had all members facing him. "Take this a little more fucking seriously," he growled out, and started to pace.

"Dom, what the fuck's wrong?" Seb stepped closer,

seeing something new in Dominic's eyes. The green had darkened, but now they were tinged with red.

"Dom, calm yourself or we can't help the female," Seb suggested, but Dominic continued to pace. Breathing deep, he slowly took back control. But only just. Lifting his chin, he looked at each warrior in turn.

"Our task is not only to escort an unclaimed and unprotected female back to Helvetia," he stated. "She is also of Rudem Crucre Regio."

Stunned, his warriors stood wide-eyed, looking at him. Then, one by one, they placed their fisted right hands over their chests. In unison, they spoke.

"She is our charge. Our life for hers."

Constance, the female he had rescued, the woman who set him aflame, was the only heir to the succubi throne. She was their queen.

Sebastian stepped closer to Dominic, his voice quiet. "How do you know?"

Dominic faced his friend. He swallowed, then answered, "I saw the mark, my friend. I am guilty of treason."

"How so?" Sebastian asked, but he already knew the answer.

"I have…" he started but bent his head instead.

"Dominic? My friend, was she consenting?" Dominic nodded in response, then spoke.

"Yes, but as soon as I saw the mark, I removed myself from the situation."

"Then there is nothing to worry about, my friend."

Dominic nodded, but guilt for touching something so special ate at him. Finally, he spoke out loud to his men. The world of the succubi would never be the same again.

"Men, let us get our queen home."

Constance jumped as she heard the door slam. She waited to see if he would walk back in and continue what he started, only he didn't. Nope, he had done the man thing; listed his orders and then walked out, leaving her body in a worse state of arousal than she had ever felt before. His touch had set her on fire, and it had been the closest she had been to an orgasm... ever.

The moment his lips had connected with her own, she had been lost. Lost to his taste and to the feel of his hands on her skin. In only a few touches, he had invaded her senses and, in essence, ruined her for all other men. Even if he was an arsehole.

She had no clue what she had done for him to push her away and act so cold, but she would use that to fuel her anger. Yes, she was grateful he had saved her life—twice—but there was no way she was going to put up being bossed around by someone she barely knew.

Constance winced. Yes, she wouldn't put up with his bullshit, but she would quite happily let him use her body. Well, as long as he made her come. Her inner perv bounced at the thought. Hell, who was she kidding; if he walked back into the room, she would most likely pounce and have her wicked way with him.

His kisses had been like a drug, something that should be made illegal. Better yet, let her bottle them so she could sell them to all the single females out there.

"Oh, fucking hell," Constance moaned quietly, and sat down on the edge of the bed. Her priorities were so screwed up. She didn't know her arse from her elbow. Since she had met Dominic, all he had seen of her was a damsel in distress, and then a tramp. She didn't blame him for changing his mind and leaving her wet and wanting. She wasn't a needy person. She had survived long enough on her own to know she didn't need anyone. Well, until earlier. But she was a woman, dammit, a strong... horny woman.

She would take no shit.

With that, Constance stood and stomped to the door. Throwing it open, she almost walked into Dominic's chest. Her pulse did its thing—speeding up until she was sure it would stutter and stop—but she didn't let that stop her. Fuelled by her *I am woman* rant, she lifted a hand and poked him hard in the chest.

"You," she poked harder, "do not get to order me around." Constance went on her tip toes and glared at the sexiest man she had ever seen, trying her best to not get distracted by the way her boobs now pressed against him. "You got that, sunshine?"

She didn't miss the widening of his eyes, before they darkened. Shit. Maybe she had pushed him too far. She had seen what he could do with some knives.

"Yes, I do," his deep voice answered, and she swore her ovaries may have burst. What was it about this man that made her body react instantaneously? He stepped forward, causing her to back up against the door, until he was right in her personal space. Again. Only he didn't look happy.

"I do because—and listen carefully, sweetheart—" he smirked down at her, and didn't that make her piss boil, "I saved your arse... twice."

Oh, for fuck sake. She was never going to live that little gem down, was she. Pushing herself away from the door, she got right back into his personal space, pressing her boobs back against him. She enjoyed it far too much when he growled. Lifting her hand again, she resumed her poking.

"You." *Poke*. "Are." *Poke*. "An." *Poke, poke, poke*. "Arse!" Frustration laced her words, and she glared into Dominic's green eyes. There was no way she was losing this little staring contest. Until a cough broke the tense silence.

"Oh shit." Constance was all she was able to say as she looked past Dominic's wide chest to see four other men standing around, all with smirks on their faces. Well, all but one. The one furthest away was outright laughing.

Her eyes snapped up to Dominic's as he growled again. Pressing his hand into her back, he pushed her a little way forward before he finally spoke.

"Constance—" he paused and then bowed his head, which made her tilt hers in response, "My lady, may I introduce the alpha team, the lead unit of enforcers to the Succubi Throne and Council."

He pushed her forward again, but this time stopped to introduce each man in her presence. It was like she had her own cast for a Dream Boy's style strip show. Each man was gorgeous, and her inner perv was going wild and throwing her knickers.

"Sebastian, my second in command." This male was just as tall as Dominic but nowhere near as wide. Long, light brown hair was tied back in a ponytail, leaving clear a regal face that wouldn't be out of place on the cover of one of those regency romance books. His dark, brown eyes, even when he smiled, held a deep sorrow that made Constance's own heart ache. She watched as he placed his right fist over his heart and bowed.

"Hail Regina." His voice filled the silence, and all Constance could do was smile and nod back. Unsure of what she be doing. Something felt very official, only she was clueless as to what.

"Alec." Dominic nodded to the next man, who stepped forward and bowed just like Sebastian had. He was slightly shorter than both Dominic and Sebastian, but what he lacked in height he made up for with width. The man was a walking tank. His eyes sparkled at her, the blue reminding her of the sea.

"Hail Regina."

"Stefan." Dominic introduced the next man, and Constance gasped. A spark of fear shooting through her, she involuntary stepped closer to Dominic, who frowned when she looked up at him. This man was tall and wide, his long dark hair reminding Constance of Viking warriors off the TV. His eyes looked dark, and she couldn't tell what colour they were. But he exuded danger. He, too, bowed.

"Hail Regina."

"And finally, we have Cooper."

This man bowed slow. Keeping his grey eyes on her, he winked, which gained a growl from Dominic. When he stood, he was taller than all the others, easily hitting the seven-foot mark. He was different. He seemed more approachable with his easy smile.

"Hail Regina."

"This is my team, Constance. They are here to protect you and escort you to Helvetia." Not giving her chance to respond, Dominic moved back and in line with his men. She watched as they all dropped to one knee and again placed their right fist over their hearts.

As one they chorused, "Our lives for yours. This we vow. With our honour, we protect you and yours. This we vow."

One by one they stood, but her eyes drifted to Dominic.

Yes, he was still hot, and yes, he was still most likely an arsehole.

"Why am I going to..." she stopped and thought. What was the name of the place again?

"Helvetia," Cooper answered her, and she snapped her finger at him before she turned and faced Dominic.

"That's the one. Yeah, why am I going there? I live here."

She watched as Dominic stepped forward and... yup, he did it again: stepped right into her personal space.

"We are taking you there because that is where you belong and where we can protect you. So, I suggest you go get that bag I asked you to pack."

"I don't take orders from you," she snapped back, and answered his glare with her own. He was really starting to get on her nerves. Nerves that were already shot to shit from the cluster fuck that had been her evening.

"If you don't go—" Dominic growled, only to be cut short by Sebastian, who placed a hand on his shoulder.

"Let me," the man said to Dominic, and without looking in her direction, Dominic walked off. Well, stomped. What was it about men; when they sulked, they stomped like four years olds. Constance's eyes followed him as if attached by some invisible thread.

"My lady, let us go back inside."

"It's Constance—or Connie." She smiled and let Sebastian lead her back into her flat. With a last look at Dominic's back, she walked through the door. Yeah, he was still an arsehole.

12

Men are Just Like Busses

CONSTANCE WENT BACK INTO HER FLAT. WALKING STRAIGHT past the guy Dominic had introduced to her as Sebastian, she perched on the arm of the sofa and folded her arms. She watched as the warrior placed his arms behind his back and paced slightly. Not that he could pace a lot; her flat was small. Constance waited for him to say something. Dominic had already explained there were demons and other beings that, before today, she believed were myth and legend only.

He had also stated that she want human either. She wanted to call bullshit on that, but everything he'd explained... it felt right. She didn't get any bad feelings, and it did explain all the random shit that had happened to her in her life.

At last, his deep voice broke the silence.

"So, what did Dominic tell you?" he asked, and pinned her with his gaze. His eyes only held warmth and kindness.

"Not much, just about demons and succubi and how I'm apparently not human." Constance shrugged, conflicting emotions sweeping through her body. She wanted to believe everything these men said, to help make sense of everything, but some of it just seemed too farfetched.

"Ok. How do you feel about that?" he asked, and Constance tilted her head as she mulled over his question. How did she feel about possibly not being human?

"Do I get super powers?" Constance asked. It was a genuine question. She watched as the warrior smirked.

Wowza. When Sebastian smiled. he was gorgeous. All the men she had been introduced to were. It was amazing how much a smile could change someone's look. Constance felt her heart jump at the thought of what Dominic would look like if he cracked a smile. Her ovaries had already exploded at the sound of his voice. A small sigh escaped her, which didn't go unnoticed by the warrior in front.

"No super powers, I'm afraid. Not like the super heroes you see on the TV. But as a succubi, you have your own little..." he paused, looking for the right word. "quirks."

"Like what? Because what I've been dealing with these past few years are not simple quirks," Constance argued. She would not go into detail again about how she was basically addicted to sex and couldn't orgasm. He didn't need to know that—hell, it bugged the hell out of her that Dominic had read her so easily.

He only nodded and smiled a little. Ah, shit. He already knew, didn't he?

"The issues you have will be sorted once we return to Helvetia."

"Right." Constance paused. "What's the catch? Why do I have to go there, when my home is here?" Constance watched the warrior and didn't miss his small wince. She watched as he took a breath, ready to tell all.

This should be good, she thought. Nothing positive ever came from a man steeling himself like that.

"As Dominic told you, we are the alpha unit, or the enforcers. The enforcers are the warriors of the succubi. There to protect the royal throne and the council."

"Yeah, he said that." Constance nodded.

"The succubi council has been in charge of the race for the past twenty-plus years because our queen died not long after her consort was killed," Sebastian explained, and Constance took it all in.

"The queen and consort had one child; a baby girl, who was the heir to the succubi throne. Only, the day the queen passed away, her child vanished and was presumed dead." He paused and looked Constance in the eye, as if willing her to accept what he was saying.

"Right, ok," she said, and watched as the big warrior sighed. He took a step forward and dropped to one knee. A stupid part of her brain, the one that cosied up with the perv, sucked in a breath. He couldn't be proposing.

Sebastian lifted his head to look up at her.

"I, Sebastian Lovell, second in command to the alphas, pledge my loyalty and life to Constance, heir apparent to the succubi throne. From this day forward, my life is yours, my sword is yours. Hail Regina."

Whoa! Constance tried to step back, only to hit the arm of the sofa. Her momentum took her over the arm and onto the seat, her legs in the air. Whatever air she had in her lungs whooshed out, along with a small scream. Although small, it created havoc.

All of the warriors who were stood outside her door now flooded into her flat, weapons drawn, ready to face down any enemy. She watched as Dominic, his face like dark thunder, lifted Sebastian from the floor and threw him against the wall, his hand around his throat.

"What the fuck did you do?"

"Nothing. She reacted to the news. Can't... breath... Dom... Get the—"

Dominic released Sebastian and moved towards Constance, his hand reaching out to pull her from the sofa. Only Constance didn't take his hand. Instead, she looked up at the ceiling as everything that had been said to her filtered through her mind.

Demons, vampyres, immortals. Succubi. Royalty...

"Constance," his deep voiced called to her.

"I'm a... I'm a..." She couldn't say the word, and as she looked up at Dominic, who leaned over the sofa, she watched as his face transformed. Gone was the anger. Instead, a smile appeared. Dear god, he had dimples. She was so screwed.

"Yes, Constance," he chuckled as she continued to perform her fish impression. "You are, in fact, a queen."

Yes, she was *so* screwed.

13

Hail Regina

DOMINIC COULDN'T HELP HIMSELF. AS MUCH AS HIS BODY WAS on fire, he had to smile as he watched Constance, their new queen, flail on the sofa. It was the most unladylike position, yet he couldn't help the chuckle that erupted from his mouth. His response was a glare, one that did nothing to stop his glee.

"Are you just going to stand there and smile, or are you going to help?" she snapped, and Dominic wiggled the fingers of the hand he had held out as soon as he had found on her back.

"Of course I will help," he paused, then added, "Your Majesty." He waited to see what her reaction would be. In the short time he had been around this feisty little female, he had grown to enjoy her little temper tantrums, and he would bet any money that to be told she was royalty just wasn't the sort of thing she wanted. He was even more pleased as she reached for his hand, and reacted.

"Shut up."

"But it's true," he said, as she got to her feet, still holding his hand, and didn't that just feel perfect. Her skin was soft, and he was desperate to continue what they had started in the bedroom. Only he knew that would now never happen.

"Just shut up, Dominic," she snapped again, and walked past him towards her bedroom. Dominic couldn't help having the last word.

"I hope you are going in there to pack... Your Majesty." His comment was rewarded by the slam of her door.

"Did you have to wind her up?" Sebastian asked as he stood next to Dominic, rubbing his throat.

"I'm sorry, my friend," Dominic immediately apologised. But when he had heard her small scream, Dominic had thought the worst.

"I would never hurt her, Dom. What the hell is going on with you?" Sebastian questioned.

"I don't know," Dominic admitted quietly. "But whatever it is, it's centred around her." It was the truth. She calmed him when he was ready to explode with rage, she made him smile even when things were serious, and she brought out every alpha instinct he had. If he didn't think it was impossible, he would be searching his hands for the bonding marks.

But that would never happen—could never happen. The queen, ruler to the succubi race, would never want a half-breed enforcer like him, and as soon as they returned her to her true home, she would find a male who would be worthy of her.

"Cooper, Alec, scout ahead. Check to see if we are going to have any more visitors. We need to get Her Majesty back to Helvetia without delay."

"Sir." Both warriors nodded before they turned and headed out of the door. Dominic watched them go before his eyes moved to the bedroom door. She pulled him, like a magnet, and Dominic really didn't want to fight it.

That kiss had been his undoing—none would compare to her from now until the day he left this world. Sighing, he turned away from the door, only to meet the sad eyes of Stefan. No words were said—they didn't need to be. Stefan had lost his own bonded centuries ago, but now and again, you could still see the pain the big warrior bore every day.

Pain Dominic, if he thought long and hard about, didn't need nor want, because that what would happen. Dominic could handle anything, had done in the past. The pain of a battle wound was nothing in comparison to what he imagined a broken heart would be, all from wanting a woman who was never his to covet.

Pacing the small flat, Dominic tried to section those feelings, needing to put them away. He didn't want nor need them.

"Fuck," he grumbled, only to stop short. Two short, sharp whistles filtered in from the open door. A further two followed.

"Shit, we have company," he growled. "Seb, Stefan..."

"On it." Both males, without being told, moved out of the flat, weapons already drawn. The whistles had come from Cooper and Alec, signalling their time had run out. They needed to get Constance back to Helvetia.

Walking to the door, Dominic contemplated knocking. It would be the gentlemanly thing to do, but then again, he had never classed himself as a gentleman. Pushing open the door, he prepared himself for an influx of swearing and shouting, only to find Constance curled up on her bed.

She looked peaceful and perfect as she slept. The dark circles below her eyes proved she had been exhausted. Slowly, Dominic approached and kneeled on the bed.

Gently, so as not to wake her, he slipped his arms under her small form and lifted her. Almost immediately, Constance nuzzled herself into his chest, her cheek resting right over his heart.

It was almost too much.

She felt perfect—too perfect. And that was wrong, but he would savour the moment whilst it lasted.

Turning, Dominic grinned. She may have begrudged him telling her what to do, but she had still done as he asked.

Stepping to the door, he bent a little and hooked a finger through the handles of the small bag she had left by the door.

It was time to get their queen home.

London being... well, London, meant it never slept. There was always something going on somewhere. At times, it was a hindrance, but right now, it helped. The crowds from a recent local gig filled the streets. Drunk and sober party-goers not ready for the night to end, continued their frivolity in the street and gave the enforcers the cover they needed. Cooper had gone ahead, making sure the way was clear. Dominic was flanked by Sebastian and Alec, with Stefan guarding his rear.

As much as he was always up for a fight, they had quickly left Constance's home and avoided any conflict. The vamps would no doubt be pissed they had managed to get away, but that wasn't his problem.

Right now, all Dominic cared about was getting the female in his arms to safety. Knowing his men had his back, Dominic had time to focus—focus on the feelings that had appeared out of blue. He was a warrior, one of the very best. He was a hunter and killer, and he showed no mercy to his enemies. He was known as the shadow, The Umbra. A title he had earned for his swift retribution to any wrongs done to his kind.

He had fought for centuries for his race, but now... Dominic looked at Constance's peaceful face. It was like his whole world had been shaken. A bit like when you shake a snow globe, only when the snow settled, it settled around her. His world now revolved around her.

He would fight for her, kill for her, and if need be, die for her.

He knew he would never experience again what it felt like to have her surrender to his kiss, feel her passion in his arms. His half-breed status would see that he would never again get this close. His heart, the dried-up husk that it was, pumped painfully in his chest. Dominic would never admit to anyone, especially this female, that she was it for him. In only a few hours, she had somehow engrained herself to his heart and attached herself to his soul.

It was too fast, but it was something he couldn't deny.

Forcing his emotions down, he sealed them away. He would protect her. But that would be all. The memory of her taste would last him for eternity.

Hearing a long, slow whistle, Dominic knew they were close to the portal. Striding out, he upped the pace, wanting to have Constance behind the doors to the palace, where he could protect her better.

"Nearly there, Dom," Sebastian called out as he moved in front. "What's the plan?" his friend asked. They had made good time getting back to the church in Whitechapel, where their portal was located. A slap in the face to those centuries before who had slaughtered his kind in the name of a deity.

"Get her settled, Seb. We will inform the council afterwards," Dominic answered. "Call Callum and request Helena's help."

Sebastian nodded and jogged in front, heading down the steps that led to the portal.

Seeing Cooper, Dominic felt himself relax, only a fraction, as he himself jogged down the steps. Dominic hated the feeling of going through the portal. It felt like hundreds of thousands of tiny pin pricks covering his entire body.

Bending his head, Dominic gritted his teeth and walked through.

Night time in Helvetia greeted him. The sky twinkled as the immortal beings that created the illusion of stars began their nocturnal gatherings. The smell of cut grass and summer filled the air. It never rained in Helvetia. Instead, it stayed in a constant state of summertime.

Pressing Constance closer to his chest, he walked through the main gates to the palace. Instead of going to the royal wing, he headed towards the main house. This was where the council and enforcers had their quarters and would be a temporary home for Constance.

His booted feet echoed along the corridor, the sound soon joined by others as his team accompanied him, before he stopped outside a plain oak door. Without knocking, he pushed inside, pleased to see his orders had been swiftly carried out.

Helena, Callum's female, had just finished making the bed and looked up. She didn't smile—she hadn't done, that he was aware, since they had brought her back. Callum had attested to the fact she was swiftly healing from her ordeal, but her eyes, that once had held an innocence, were now serious.

"Place her on the bed, please, my lord. I will tend to her."

Dominic quickly moved around the bed. He was reluctant to release the burden in his arms, liking the way, even in sleep, she clung to him. Forcing himself, Dominic placed her within the pillows, waiting until the last possible moment to stop touching her. As he stood, he turned towards Helena.

"You will look after her?"

"Yes, my lord. My mate has told me of her importance."

"Thank you. There will be a guard outside at all times—one of the alphas. No one else is to see or talk to her."

"Yes, my lord."

Nodding once more, he looked down at Constance. He clenched his fists in an attempt to stop himself from reaching down and sliding his fingers over her cheek. She was not his to touch, no matter how much he wanted to.

Turning, he walked out of the door. Shutting it firmly, he faced his brothers.

"Alec, you have first watch."

"Yes, Dom," he answered, and took his place by the door.

Sebastian, Cooper, and Stefan faced him, waiting for his orders.

"I need to inform Michael." he stated simply, and all nodded. He didn't miss the crinkle of eyes as they held back a smile.

"He will not like this, Dominic," Stefan, the usually quiet one, said, his usually slight accent thick.

"No, he won't," Dominic agreed. "But he will accept it."

"Are you definitely sure she is—" Sebastian started, only to be interrupted.

"Yes, Seb, she is. She bears the mark."

"Well, shit's going to get a little more entertaining around here, then," Cooper shot out, before he held his hands up as both Dominic and Sebastian glared.

"Just stating a fact. You know that bastard likes to be in charge." When no one answered him and only continued to glare, he sighed. "Fine. I'm gonna go and find Callum before my watch starts. God, can you guys get any more bloody grumpy!" With that, Cooper turned and walked down the corridor, soon followed by Stefan.

"He's right, you know," Sebastian sighed.

"Yeah, she will need all the help she can get." Dominic looked at the door. Their whole world was about to change, but not as much as hers. A part of him worried that she would reject what she had been told. Reject her heritage.

There was more at stake than her simply taking the throne. Their race depended on her.

"Come, let us deliver the news," Dominic stated, and started down the corridor. Alec chuckled when Sebastian sighed again.

"You are going to enjoy this, aren't you?" Sebastian asked as he moved to catch up.

"Damn right, I am. Nothing makes me happier than seeing that tosser lose his shit." Dominic stopped and faced his friend.

"He's going to lose it... big time."

14

Council Dealings

MICHAEL DREAMED OF POWER. IT WAS WHAT HE CRAVED AND relished. It was what drove him and what made making those difficult decisions worth doing. The race—his race—was doomed, and he really couldn't care less. So he would make sure he was settled for the duration of his immortality and would watch the rest burn.

That was the plan. Only the enforcers, mainly those who were loyal to the alphas, made his job that little bit more difficult. But with females being bonded where he chose them to be and others going missing... Michael sniggered. The race would no longer believe in the enforcers to protect them. Would no longer want a half-breed prick like Dominic to lead their warriors.

All Michael had to do was bide his time.

Like he did with the queen and her consort.

Soon, all would be his.

The loud knock on the door pulled Michael from his fantasies. He growled under his breath as he moved from the bed to a large armchair that sat in front of a large fireplace. His room was decadent, filled with items that showed his wealth and power.

"Enter," he called out, although he didn't look as they entered. Instead, he looked into the flames, watched as his plans of glory took shape and played out.

"My lord."

"What is it?"

"The alphas," his guards started. Michael hated the alphas. Hated them with a passion that bordered on insanity. They were the proverbial thorn in his side, and he couldn't wait to have them all exterminated.

He had to be patient.

"What about the alphas?" he snapped, and finally looked into the guard's face. He was young. Easier to manipulate.

"They request to see you. Urgently."

"Who's 'they'," Michael snapped.

"Dominic and Sebastian."

"Oh, really..." Michael snorted. He took enjoyment over the fact they had come running to him. Nodding to the guard, he continued. "Very well, show them into the office, please," Michael said in a pleasant voice.

The guard's eyes widened in surprise before he bowed and left the room. The urge to tell the guard to inform the alphas he was busy had nearly won. But a chance to gloat over them was an opportunity he couldn't miss.

Since the royal line had been wiped out and Michael had taken over, the alphas hadn't seemed... Well, they had never seen eye to eye. They wanted the royal line back, and he didn't.

He was the leader of the race now, not some whore of a woman who had chosen a mate below her. She had brought ridicule to the race. She was better off gone. The royal line a joke to the title.

Whatever the enforcers wanted, Michael would enjoy watching them squirm. Slipping on a silk robe, he walked out of his bedroom and into his office, a smile on his face. He would enjoy knocking Dominic Carlisle down a few pegs.

He would enjoy watching him die even more, but that would have to wait.

Patience, Michael reminded himself. *Patience*.

Dominic knew he was scowling but couldn't bring himself to care. The office of Michael was filled with expensive furniture and paintings. Material things that would have cost more than all the enforcers' meagre wages combined. But that wasn't what annoyed him.

No, the male himself was an arse, and Dominic hated him. They had never gotten on. Why should they? Dominic fought to protect his race. Michael only seemed to want to destroy it. Since he had become the self-appointed ruler, he had cared little for the lives of the lower-class succubi, instead focusing only on the upper-class and forcing bonds. Their race, due to this, was dying.

There were hardly any births anymore. There were hardly any females.

And what had this jumped up tosser done? Ignored it to suit his own gain. So the news Dominic was about to deliver was going to bring him, he hoped, to his knees.

"Dominic," Sebastian warned as he stood shoulder to shoulder with him

"What?" he asked, although he knew what was going to be said.

"Try looking... I don't know, less like you want to rip his head off."

Dominic raised an eyebrow but didn't saying anything. Both males turned at the sound of a door opening.

In walked the man of the hour. Michael was a greasy-looking male. That was the only way to describe him. Dark hair slicked back, his frame was broad, but he lacked bulk. His hands were soft from the lack of doing anything that could possibly cause him to sweat.

In Dominic's eyes, this male let his race down both in deed and appearance. Not one to get his hands dirty, he preferred to delegate the dirty jobs.

"What do I owe the pleasure?" Michael asked as he slid into his chair. His silk robe billowed out, showing off a pale, bare chest.

"We have come to inform you that a female, an unprotected one at that, was located and returned to Helvetia by the alpha team," Dominic said strongly, knowing he was prolonging the conversation. He wanted to draw it out, if only to make the councilman in front of him squirm.

"Ahh, very good. Is that all?" Michael stood.

"No," Dominic stated again.

"Oh. Very well, continue." He lazily waved his hand.

"The female has been raised human and has no idea about the existence of immortals, never mind what she is."

"Then why the hell did you bring her back? She is of no use to the race," Michael sneered, and Dominic could tell the councilman's patience was wearing thin.

"I brought her back because she is a succubi female, and as such, deserves our protection," Dominic snapped.

"Fine. See that she is dealt with, then. Why you had to

inform me, I don't know. I have better things to do than sit and listen to an enforcer."

Dominic's hands fisted, and as he looked to Sebastian, he could see his friend felt the same contempt for the sorry excuse for a male in front of them. They had already sworn themselves to the protection and loyalty of Constance, but now, without words being spoken, they vowed to make sure she was crowned Queen. Anyone would be better at leading the race than him.

"I'm sorry, but I thought you should be made aware," Dominic started, and bowed his head before he turned and moved towards the door. Sebastian already there. Before he walked through, he stopped and turned his head, pinning Michael with a look.

"Although, the female isn't just any female," he started.

"Oh really?" Michael sneered. "Another pretty pussy, no doubt."

Dominic growled, "Not at all."

"So, what is it, then, Dominic? I don't have all day."

Dominic smirked. "She bears the mark, Michael." He sneered his name and watched as the male's eyes widened. "Our queen has returned."

Not staying to witness Michael's reaction, he left the room, his long strides catching up with Sebastian.

"You enjoyed that far too much," his friend said.

"Not as much as I would enjoy having my fist meet intimately with his face," Dominic answered, then sobered. "We need to guard her. He won't give up power easily."

"Not to worry, Dom. We will keep her safe."

Dominic nodded. They could keep her safe, protect her. He just hoped he could protect her from himself.

15

New Beginnings. New Friends

GENTLE SINGING WAS THE FIRST THING THAT FILTERED through Constance's mind. Her consciousness struggled to break through, instead lingering in that place between asleep and awake. The sweet sound, instead of lulling her back into the comfort of darkness, made her curious. The last thing she remembered was being surrounded by Dominic's strength, only now she was on a soft surface. Comfortable. Warm. She ached, who wouldn't after the event she had been through. The bruises would fade as would the memories. She was alive and that was what mattered

Constance opened her eyes slowly. No harsh lights met her gaze. Instead, the lighting was dimmed. the golden glow from the lamps giving a sense of warmth. Her eyes quickly scanned the room before falling on the back of a woman. Dark hair fell in waves around her shoulders as she bent to whatever task she was doing. She was dressed in a gown of deep blue, the kind of dress you only saw in those period dramas on the TV.

Constance kept quiet for a moment. The events before she had crashed washed over her. Events that now meant the life she had known was over. According to Dominic, she wasn't human. She was like him; an immortal being. Getting her head around the information was almost mind numbing. Before she'd met Dominic, the idea of immortals, vampyres, and even demons, was only something she had either read about or seen on the TV. Add to that, Dominic and Sebastien were convinced she was royalty.

Not just any royalty, but the queen.

A part of Constance—in fact, most of Constance—would like to call bullshit. Only, something about the situation felt right as much as it sounded wrong. These succubi warriors, if anything, would be able to help her understand what was going on with her. Maybe even have something to help. Dominic had said he could help.

Memories of his hands and lips on her back in her flat zipped through her mind and heated her from the inside. In such a short space of time, that man had her body responding to the very thought of him. If only he hadn't stopped. Constance may have been able to get some sort of relief.

"Ahh, you are awake." The woman had turned around and was now looking down at Constance, who, being wrapped up in her own thoughts, had missed her approach and her questions.

"I'm sorry, what?"

"I am glad to see you are finally awake, my lady." Constance watched as the lady dipped into a small curtsey.

"My name is Helena, and I am here to assist you."

Constance looked at her new companion. With hair that

fell to her shoulders, it shimmered in the dull light. Her face was beautiful, in a classical sort of way. Her blue eyes sparkled as they crinkled at the edges. She was a similar height to Constance, although she would kill to have the curves Helena was rocking. Her hands caught Constance's attention.

She had nails that were perfectly manicured, but her gaze was drawn to the dark marks that covered her hands. They were stark against her pale skin. Without looking closer, Constance couldn't make out the pattern, although it reminded her of the mandalas she'd seen in those relaxing colouring books.

"They are my mating marks, my lady." Helena's voice once again pulled Constance from the trap of her own thoughts. Constance frowned.

"They appeared when I bonded with my mate. The stronger the bond, the darker the mark." Constance watched as Helena moved her hands, looking at her own marks. The smile on her face was something Constance envied. This woman was clearly in love.

"Right," Constance finally spoke. "Nice to meet you, Helena." Pushing up on her hands, Constance moved so she could sit upright. As much as Helena seemed like a lovely woman, there was one person she wanted to see, and he wasn't here.

"Where is Dominic?" Constance asked. She tried to avoid sounding needy, but she was. The need to see him—to smell him—was shockingly powerful. She had never in her life reacted to any man like that. It wasn't right. It wasn't normal.

But then again, Constance had been told only a few hours ago that she wasn't normal. The term was overrated anyway.

"My lady, he has gone with his second to see the council and inform them of your arrival. That is also why I am here."

Disappointment coursed through Constance as the need pulsed and became stronger. It was similar to the one she had struggled with most of her life, only now it was focused on one thing. On one man.

Dominic.

Constance shook her head and tried to focus. She watched as Helena continued to talk as she moved about the room, pulling a large amount of fabric from a chest at the base of the bed.

"I am here to prepare you to meet the council, and also to talk you through any questions you might have."

"Why?" she asked simply.

"As the heir, you will have to meet the council. They have been the ones in charge, and, as such, will need clarification that you are who you say you are."

Constance frowned. "What kind of clarification?"

"Firstly, they will ask to see your mark, and secondly, your blood will confirm or deny your birth right."

"Right," Constance answered again, her mind a whirlpool. Her thoughts took her back to the woman she had always thought was her mother. The same woman who had been sat in St. Joseph's since Constance was fourteen, ranting about demons and vampyres.

The day she was abandoned to a life with no family and no idea how to survive. Yet she had... just.

"The council is led by Michael." Constance didn't miss the anger in Helena's tone as she mentioned that name. Or the fact she gripped the fabric in her hands tightly. Any harder and the material would rip.

"What's wrong with him?" Constance asked, showing a small smile as Helena looked up at her.

"I'm sorry, my lady. Who?"

"Michael," Constance stated, and watched for Helena's reaction. The woman lowered her head as if to avoid eye contact and busied herself by fussing over the material she had pulled from the chest. As its bulk unfolded, Constance could now see it was a stunningly beautiful dress of burnished gold.

"Nothing is wrong with him, my lady," Helena answered, but her voice wavered slightly, giving away a hint of what Constance would guess was fear. Fear was something Constance understood. In her short life, she had at one time been a prisoner of her own fear. But being left to fend for yourself at fourteen would do that.

What was it they said... 'It was a dog eat dog world', so Constance had made sure she was up on the food chain and not an easy target. That being said, she could spot the signs a mile away.

"Helena," she called out, eager to pull her newfound friend from whatever demons she was fighting. She waited until her bright blue eyes met her own.

"Is Michael someone I should be wary of?" she asked bluntly.

"My lady, it is not my place—" Helena started to answer, but Constance interrupted her.

"Let me stop you there, honey," Constance began. "Helena. Listen. If I'm honest, I'm out of my depth right now. Hell, I didn't even know beings like vamps and demons existed outside of fairy tales. Everything that has happened has come as a bit of a shock, and then you guys drop the Q bomb on me, I feel like I don't know my arse from my elbow." Constance smiled and tilted her head as she continued. "Right now, I feel like I'm alone."

"But you are not alone. You have me." Helena finally smiled, and Constance watched as her whole being shone. "You also have the enforcers."

"That's true," Constance agreed. "But I need to know who I can trust. You were born in this world, right?"

"Yes, my lady." Constance smiled, but this time it was because Helena had slowly relaxed and had now left the gown to sit on the edge of the bed, closer to Constance.

"So, you will know the ins and outs of succubi politics."

"I guess."

"So that means you can guide me." Constance paused. "Michael? Can I trust him?"

Constance's eyes never left Helena as she asked her question, looking for anything that would help her understand the world she had been thrust into. She needed allies, ones who knew the game that she was yet to learn.

"No," Helena finally answered honestly. "I would not trust that male."

"Good, then I don't trust him." Constance fought an inner war. One side urged her to ask again about Dominic, and the other told her to stop wanting a man who clearly had never wanted her. Not really.

The latter lost.

"Can I trust Dominic?"

At the mention of the man's name, Helena smiled. "My lady, that is one male who would give up his life and his very soul for you. Yes, you can trust him."

Butterflies erupted as if they were taking flight in her stomach at hearing the vow. Her imagination took the words and turned them into a scene where she pictured Dominic on his knees. He filled every thought. In a short time, her body was so attuned to his presence that when he wasn't near, it mourned the loss.

"Right." Constance coughed, her body once again on edge. "That's good to know." Her voice had become husky with desire. Why did she react this way to only the thought of the man?

"The enforcers are good males, my lady. Each one would give their lives for your own. Even my Callum."

Helena's voice broke whatever spell the memory of Dominic had, and Constance nodded in response. She pushed the covers away from her legs and swung them over the side. As she stood, she rolled her shoulders.

"I take it we don't have much time."

"No. I am sorry."

"We had best get started, then. You have much to teach me and not a lot of time to do it." Constance ignored the panic that threatened to take over. This was her world now, there was no room for panic, no room for freaking out. In short, she had to man the fuck up and deal.

The succubi wanted a queen—thought her to be that queen.

She would hate to disappoint them.

_____

16

The Test of Royalty

Dominic paced the small foyer that lead to the main council chamber. It had been a good few hours since he had last seen Constance, and he felt irritable. He couldn't settle, so instead, he paced across the garish, red-patterned carpet under the watchful gaze of Sebastian and Stefan.

His second was leaning against the wall, large arms crossed as he whistled a random tune. Whereas Stefan stood on guard like the true Viking he was. His team of enforcers were the best. He was proud of each and every one of them. They protected their race with honour and skill few other races could match.

They had been his family, all he knew. Until now.

He would always put his race first, protect them and his men with his life, but now he had someone more important to protect. He was in no doubt that Constance was the rightful ruler of their race. Her mark declared it. Hell, he felt it—not just in his gut, but deeper. Right down to the pit of his soul.

She was now his to protect. But that was all it could be for a being like him. Even if he wanted more.

His thoughts scattered as the doors opened. The woman he had left tucked up in bed was a world away from what he saw now.

Constance had been dressed as her station dictated.

"*Fuck.*" The curse flew from his mouth, and with it came the breath he hadn't realised he held. She was an angel—that was the only word that could come close to the vision that stood in front of him. Dominic's eyes travelled down her body and back up again in an attempt to take it all in.

Dressed in a gown of burnished gold, she radiated grace and elegance. The dress was a traditional gown with flowing skirts and a rounded neckline, showing off the delicate curve of her neck. Her long, dark hair had been styled to perfection. The curls fell to her shoulders, but most of her hair had been pinned up. Helena had made what was to him the most stunning woman he had ever seen, into a goddess. One he would happily worship for eternity.

The rustle of her skirts was the only sound that filled the small room. The world itself narrowed down to encompass only the two of them as his green eyes connected with her blue ones. Energy sizzled between them, forging a connection Dominic was unable to deny.

But he had to. The woman who now stood in front of him was their queen. She was forbidden, no matter what body and soul told him. Glancing down briefly, he looked at his hands, hopeful he would see the markings that signalled he had met his mate. But as expected, nothing was there.

Stepping forward, Dominic dropped to one knee, followed by both Sebastian and Stefan.

"Your Highness, the alpha team are at your service." Dominic kept his head bowed, not trusting himself to look at Constance directly. The need for her—to hold her, kiss her—was becoming almost unbearable.

"Thank you," Constance answered, and Dominic could no longer resist the pull. Standing, he allowed himself to look into her eyes. She looked calm, if not for the wariness in her eyes.

Holding out his arm, he offered it to her.

"Don't leave me alone." Her whisper was meant for his ears only, and his chest swelled at the trust she had in him.

"Never," he replied, and nodded to his men to open the door. This meeting would be a test for not only Constance, but for his men as well. Their world that had once been sedate, would now have purpose and meaning. They would protect their queen no matter the cost.

Dominic knew Michael would not go out easily. The man craved power, and it had been left unchecked for far too long. That, in a way, had been the enforcers' fault. They let him take over the council and proclaim himself leader. But they'd had little choice. When their queen had died, it left the whole race in turmoil. So as much as Dominic hated to admit it, Michael had at least done one thing right. He had kept the race going.

But it was time for the councilman to step down and let the rightful heir take her place. Constance's hand increased its pressure on his arm, the only sign that she was nervous. Patting her hand with his own, he squeezed a little, showing her his support.

"My lords of the council, may I present to you Lady Constance Carlisle, daughter and heir apparent to Queen Ena and Queen's Consort, Alvars."

Sebastian's voice was cloud and clear, and quiet descended upon the council. Slowly, Dominic releases Constance's arm. He turned and bowed to her, before he stepped back into a protective position. He hated to leave her alone. The panic in her eyes had been fleeting, but he then saw resolve and a strength that filled him again with hope. But this time, it was hope for the race.

Her heels clicked against the marble floor as she stepped into the middle of the room. With a visible deep breath, her lyrical voice filled the room.

"My lord councilmen, I come before you as the daughter to Queen Ena and Queen's Consort, Alvars. I am here to claim the throne that is mine by right." Dominic was entranced at Constance's words, words that held authority and strength. He watched as she turned her back to the council and moved the array of curls from her left shoulder. Due to the style of the dress, she didn't need to move any material to show off the birthmark that was stark against her skin. The star was clear. She bore the mark. She was the rightful queen.

"I bear the mark of my bloodline," she stated simply, and turned back to face the lords. Silence filled the room before quiet whispers started. Lords leaned in to whisper in others' ears. Dominic watched each and every one, as did his men, looking for any sign that Constance was in danger. He focused on Michael, who was sat on the throne. The small smirk that played on his lips made Dominic's jaw tick.

"My lady," Michael called out, instantly silencing the room again. He stood in one motion, his cloak floating out behind him as he moved from the raised platform where the simple throne stood.

"Welcome to our council, and welcome home to Helvetia." He stopped mere feet away from Constance, and Dominic fought every instinct he had to not place her behind him. The councilman didn't hide his pleasure at looking at Constance, taking his time to look up and down her body, obvious desire in his eyes. For that, Dominic couldn't blame him. She was breath-taking.

"Thank you, councilman," she answered coldly, becoming the role of regal queen Dominic knew she could be. He wanted to smirk at her indifference to him but kept his face devoid of emotion.

"Please, call me Michael. I have a feeling we will have a lot to do with each other." Michael's voice changed as he turned on the charm.

"I would rather not, and yes, we no doubt will," she quickly stated, again surprising Dominic with her ability to rebound the councilman's charms. "I would like to go to the royal wing now. As you can probably tell, there is a lot to do."

Dominic wanted to laugh at the shocked look on Michael's face as she spoke down to him, before she turned and then looked Dominic in the eye. Ready to do her bidding, he stepped forward and offered his arm, feeling ten-feet-tall when she placed hers around his. Before moving off, she looked over her shoulder to the still shell-shocked Michael.

"I'm assuming you want to authenticate my claim to the throne. What better way for it to be done than gaining entry to my mother's suite?" She paused and waited for Michael to nod. "Fabulous. Shall we?" She faced front again, and Dominic was happy to see the small smile that crossed her face. His men, already leading, left the council room.

Constance was a force to be reckoned with, that he was certain of. Her ability to quickly assess a situation and think on her feet was a great start to her reign. Her whispered voice pulled him from his thoughts as they moved down the corridor.

"Was that alright?" Her words were breathy, and he felt her hands shake. But only a little.

"Perfect," he responded, and watched as her face lit up and the hand that lay on his forearm gripped slightly.

"You are a natural," he whispered back. "And look absolutely stunning." The words fell from his lips, but he wouldn't retract them. Not when she looked at him with such wonder.

"Really?"

"Really." Dominic would do anything within his power to keep the look of happiness that filtered across her face. Hell, he would move the earth itself to keep her happy. This woman, their queen, had somehow, in a short space of time, burrowed beneath his skin, beneath the ice he had locked around his half-breed heart and made a home there.

And suddenly Dominic didn't care anymore. She filled a void in his soul that he hadn't realised had been empty. He would live happily with the fact she could never be his, as long as he could protect her.

His life for hers. As it should be.

17

Strength Within

CONSTANCE WAS A BAG OF NERVES INSIDE. HER STOMACH WAS doing more flips than a gymnastics athlete, but without the finesse. If she had anything in her stomach, it would have come up. The only thing that kept her grounded was Dominic.

It had sent tingles coursing through her when their eyes had met. She hadn't missed the widening of his green orbs when he had seen her. Helena had done a grand job of making her look the part of Queen. But it had been Dominic's approval she had sought.

Constance had wanted to place her hand on her heaving chest when Dominic had gotten down on one knee. A bit like those cheesy regency movies, just before the hero sweeps his love off her feet.

But this wasn't a movie; this was her life now. So she had done exactly what Helena had told her to do.

Act like an indifferent bitch, because for some reason, the councilmen to this race couldn't deal with it and would expect her to be all meek and quiet. That wasn't her at all, and acting a bitch would be easy. Especially with her enforcers there as well.

Entering the hall had been an eye opener. Marble, lined with veins of gold, was everywhere. The room itself was circular with large wooden seats placed at even intervals around the outside. Opposite the entrance was an alcove that held a large marble seat. The marble was outmatched by the gold. The chandeliers above meant any flecks of the precious metal sparkled. On this seat had sat the infamous Michael.

Constance was in no doubt he had deliberately placed himself on the throne, a sign of his power at the moment. Helena had told her how she felt about the man—or male, as they were referred to. He wanted control, craved it, so as expected, would be reluctant to give it up. Even to the true heir. A part of Constance was worried that her mark was just that: a mark that had no meaning.

But deep down, she knew it wasn't as simple as just a mark. Everything about what she had been told, felt right. Helena had schooled her well on what to say, and she would be daft to not admit she loved seeing the slight shock on the face of Michael when she hadn't succumbed to his attempt at charm.

When he had stood from the throne and walked towards her, she had to stop herself from snorting. He was dressed in an outfit that, again, wouldn't be out of place in a regency movie, only times the frills by ten. That, coupled with a cloak... he looked ridiculous. Constance had fought hard to suppress the shiver of unease when he took his time to look her up and down, and she hadn't missed the flare of desire in his eyes. That right there had made her want to heave. The male set her nerves on edge, and whatever he thought was charm was more along the lines of being creepy.

His build was slender. In fact, he was half the size of Dominic, with dull, grey eyes and black hair that was slicked back from his face. He was as different from Dominic as night was from day, and her gut feeling was agreeing with Helena's assessment. He wasn't someone to be trusted.

So, she had said her piece and stated her intentions, and now was on the way to prove her claim by gaining entrance to the royal suites. When the queen had died, as was custom, the suite had been locked. The only way for anyone to gain entrance was through the giving of blood. Royal blood. Only those who were an heir could open them, and it was also a test, so no one could falsely claim the throne.

Mixed emotions flowed through Constance as she gripped Dominic's arm for strength. Excitement at the prospect of finally finding out the truth of where she came from and what she was thrilled through her, yet alongside that ran dread. Uncertainty wormed its way in. What if this was all just a big mistake? Would she get arrested? What would happen?

"My lady," Michael called as he quickened his pace so he was able to walk beside her. Unconsciously, she gripped Dominic's arm tighter.

"Let me be the one to escort you. You have no need for the enforcers within your own home." Michael smiled, but there was no kindness behind it.

"I thank you, councilman, but *my* enforcers go where I go. This is not yet my home, but don't worry, it will be." Constance gave the male a small nod but nothing else, hoping he would take the hint and leave her alone. He made her skin crawl.

Instead, he only smiled again. "Very well, if that is your wish."

Constance nodded again and waited for the male to back off, moving to walk behind Sebastian and Stefan, who followed close behind. Knowing they were there helped to calm her nerves, but only slightly.

"Where are the others?" Constance asked, wanting to fill the silence. She had been alone for so long, she craved to speak to people.

"Cooper and Alec are already outside the suites. Callum is with Helena. They don't do well being apart for very long. Are you ok?"

Constance nodded again and rolled her eyes. That was all she seemed to do lately. Smiling slightly, she looked up at Dominic. "Yes, I think so. It's just a lot to deal with."

"You are doing amazing." His praise brought back the butterflies and helped fight back the panic. It was strange how one male's words could make her skin crawl, and yet another could soothe her like a cooling balm. Want, need, even affection filled her as she looked at his green eyes. Something within their depths caught her and held on.

"There is red in your eyes. I never noticed before," Constance blurted as she leaned closer, eager to see. Only to have Dominic stop. His face changed, becoming a cold mask that made Constance feel like she had been hit in the gut.

"It's nothing. Come, we must keep moving."

The change in his demeanour annoyed Constance. One minute, she felt like he liked her, desired her. The next, she felt like he couldn't stomach to be in her presence. Yet, even with all that, she was drawn to him.

You could say she was drawn much like bugs to one of those electric zappers. If she got too close, she was going to get hurt. She let a sigh escape her lips as he moved them faster down the corridor, only slowing slightly when a pair of large ornate doors came in to view.

Yes, she was drawn to him like a moth to a flame. If she got burned, though, would it be worth it?

Michael slowly seethed inside. He had never hated anyone like he did Dominic, but right now, the new wannabe queen was heading to be top of the list. He had expected a small, quiet female, one that he could control—and maybe fuck. She was beautiful, after all, and would, like any succubi female, be a better than average lay.

Hell, he was even considering the whole mating idea—a sure-fire way to keep his grip on the throne that was his. He had earned it after all.

She had dismissed him when he had offered his services. It was clear she didn't like him, which meant getting rid of her would now be a pleasure.

But no, she had to be one of those confident, bitchy women who thought for themselves. He shuddered. This Constance had already managed to gain the loyalty of the enforcers—not that they were ever on his side. What made him laugh was Dominic's keen interest in the female. That male wasn't worthy of any female, with him being a pathetic half-breed. Yet, seeing him bow down to a woman would have its merits.

Only Michael would not be doing the same.

There was a chance she may fail the next text. After all, anyone could have a mark. Tattooists were quite the artists these days, but only the blood of the true heir could gain entry.

Either way, Michael had work to do. He needed allies to

help him keep control of the succubi race, and the other councilmen would now back the queen. None of them had any back bone, anyway.

He didn't need them. What he needed was someone else who wanted power, like him. Michael smirked from behind the enforcers as they approached the royal suite's doors.

The doors dated back hundreds of years and had been be spelled by the fae. In the centre of the doors was a carved circle. If he had cared for such things, Michael would have marvelled at the craftsmanship. But he didn't care. The only thing he cared about was what was on the other side of that door.

There was no one left alive who knew the real reason for the early deaths of the queen and her consort, and he planned to keep it that way. The chance that something had been left to implicate him was high, but he would have to wait and see how things played out.

Michael hated not being in control, but it was temporary. Just like the new queen in front.

He would make sure of that.

18

Inheritance

Constance looked up at the ornate and imposing door. The woodwork had been hand-carved and was so intricate it would take hours, if not days, to study. What was most important, though, was the carved circle in the middle. It was about the size of a dinner plate and had a Celtic knot pattern around the edges. Inside was a handprint-sized indent.

"My lady." Both Cooper and Alec stood on either side. They went to one knee and placed a fist over their heart.

"Constance." Dominic's whispered word pulled her gaze to his. It surprised her as he hadn't said her name since they were in her flat.

"Helena told you what to do?" he asked quietly, making sure they couldn't be heard by Michael and the other councilmen behind.

"Yes," she confirmed, and then turned to face the door

again. Cracking her neck—which was the most unladylike habit she had—Constance stepped forward. She ignored the panic that threatened to take over and sent a silent prayer to whoever might be listening.

Reaching forward, she placed her right palm within the indent. Tingles shot up her hand as soon as it touched the wood. Forcing herself to keep her hand in place, she closed her eyes and recited the words Helena had taught her.

"Sanguine Meo Quod Aperire Ianuam." *By my blood, open this door.*

Silence reined, and Constance felt her heart drop. What would happen to her now?

A slight click sounded, snapping Constance's gaze to where her hand rested against the wood. Another click could be heard, and Constance felt sharpness against her entire hand, almost like small pinpricks from the base of her palm all the way up to her fingertips.

Constance gasped, but before she was able to complain, a whirring began, followed by loud clunks. Before her eyes, and those of the councilmen and the enforcers, the door to the royal suite opened, leaving Constance stood with her hand still in the air.

Turning, she looked first to Dominic, who, shockingly, grinned back at her before he dropped to one knee and placed his fist over his heart. He was soon followed by the rest of the enforcers, and the councilmen. Last, though, was Michael, who looked at her with pure hate before he masked his true feelings and smiled. Then, he, too, dropped to one knee.

"Hail Regina," was chorused, the latin for queen echoed through the corridor. Constance's gaze locked down on her palm. Small spots of blood could be seen from the multiple pricks, but under all of that was now a pattern. Circular on the palm. It resembled the Celtic pattern on the door. The pattern continued up each finger.

"It is the mark of a succubi. All receive it when they reach maturity. Somehow, the magic knew you had been missing from us. It will also expand and darken when you find you bonded mate." Dominic answered her silent question before he turned and addressed the councilmen.

"As you can now see, she is confirmed the lost daughter of Queen Ena and Consort Alvars." Without waiting for a response, Dominic turned Constance and pushed her towards the room.

"Come, this suite hasn't been open in many years. I will call for Helena, so she may assist you." Constance let herself be pushed into the room. Her enforcers followed behind as the councilmen left to deliver the news to the rest of the race, and to the other races who called Helvetia home.

Only Michael remained.

"My lady, I know you have a great deal to do, so I won't keep you. I would like the enforcers to head back to the surface," he stated broadly, and gained everyone's attention. Only, it wasn't her that answered.

"For what purpose, councilman?" Dominic demanded.

"I have received news that another installation has been found." Constance tilted her head and watched the male. Something didn't sit right, but she couldn't put her finger on it.

Before Dominic could answer, Constance stepped in. She had dealt with enough arsehole men to know that if she didn't stand up for herself and stake her authority now, he would try to undermine her at every opportunity.

"Councilman Michael, thank you for divulging this information. If you could give any details to Sebastian, I would be most grateful. Only then can we assign the proper men for the task."

"But... they should go now," he argued, seemingly flustered,

"To what gain? Are they aware we know?" she asked, and was rewarded with silence. He was trying his hardest stop her and the enforcers going into the suite, but she hadn't a clue for what reason.

"Right." She stopped and eyed the councilman "Please give Sebastian the information. You are dismissed."

When he had left, she watched as Cooper shut the door. "Do I want to know what that was about?" she asked Dominic, who just grinned at her, along with Stefan, Cooper and Alec.

"What?" she asked, but didn't get an answer. Throwing her hands in the air, she turned and walked down the short corridor. Men—bloody pain in the arses, the lot of them, no matter what the race.

On the walls were portraits of queens from times past. Each one was stunningly depicted and had her own blue eyes staring back at her. These were her ancestors, the women whose blood ran through her veins.

The small corridor opened into a large sitting room, with multiple doors that led from it. A huge fireplace took over an entire wall, and above it, another portrait, only this one drew her in.

A queen sat proudly, dressed in reds and golds, and behind her stood a tall male with dark eyes. He was not dressed like the queen—in a regal way that would befit his station. Instead, he wore all black; black shirt, black trousers. On his forearms he wore braces, and across his chest was a leather harness. Above his left shoulder was the hilt of a sword. He stood just behind the queen, his hand on her shoulder.

Familiarity filled her as she looked at the face of the male, and then moved over to the female, only to gasp. Her likeness looked back at her. Same eyes, nose, mouth... Even the length of hair and the way it was worn was the same.

"Shit," Constance breathed as her hand went to her mouth.

A small label on the bottom left hand side pulled her gaze.

Queen Ena and her husband, Queen's Consort Alvars.

Dominic couldn't—wouldn't—take his gaze from Constance as she moved about the royal suite. Both he and the other enforcers had been impressed by how she dealt with Michael. None of them had stopped grinning when he had been dismissed.

Nearly every enforcer had been subjected to the male and his holier than thou attitude. He had made it quite clear that they would not be allowed to bond with any female, unless he allowed it, wanting to save the females for the males he had chosen, and, in essence, forcing a bond. That was why the arrival of Constance was so important. With her in charge, the forced bondings would be halted, and true bonds would be given a chance to take place. Thus ensuring the survival of the succubi race.

It was a lot to place on a single person's shoulders, but they had little choice. Constance was the true queen. He had seen the confidence and strength she possessed. He was in awe of her.

"Shit." Her quiet curse had him moving to her side

immediately. He found her looking up at a portrait of her parents.

"You ok?"

"That's them," she answered, her eyes never leaving the portrait.

"Yes, it is. This was done not long after they found out they were expecting you," he explained, and then lifted his hand and pointed to where the consort and queen's hands met on her shoulders.

"I never saw marks as dark as theirs. Their bond was so strong, and they loved each other with their entire soul."

"What happened to them?" Constance asked Dominic, and he was unable to deny her request, as upsetting as the story was.

"I don't know the full details. I was not privy to any information at that time," Dominic started. "The Queens Consortwas the leader of the enforcers then, taking charge, and even though he was king, he still went out on missions. He led by example, and was who I wanted to emulate as a youngster. Out on a simple mission, his team was ambushed. There are mixed reports as to who was responsible. Some say vamps, others say the weres. When news reached the mansion, chaos ensued.

"The queen, who had not long given birth to you, she was inconsolable and secluded herself to her suite, only dealing with her ladies in waiting."

Dominic reached out and wiped a tear away from Constance's face with his thumb, that small touch fuelling his already intense need to take her in his arms.

"Not long after her seclusion, we were informed of her death. Some say she died of a broken heart, and when we asked about you, we were informed you had perished with your mother."

Reluctantly, he removed his hand. Her face was the spitting image of her mothers, yet he could see the strength she had gained from her father radiating from her.

"That is all I know—that is all anyone knows."

He watched as Constance nodded.

"Who informed the enforcers and the race of this information?" she asked as she moved back to the painting. In a sweet gesture, she kissed her fingers and reached up, laying them at the feet of her mother and father.

"It was Michael. He was head of the council and, as such, would take over if something should happen to the royal family," he answered, something that had been well known. Yet it was only now that information felt wrong, like something didn't add up.

"Thought as much." Constance's reply was short, and he didn't follow her as she moved away from him. She moved to explore each room on her own. Turning, he found Sebastian, Stefan, Cooper and Alec watching him.

"Is she ok?" Cooper asked.

"As well as can be expected. It's a lot to take in for someone not from our world."

"True, but she's stronger than she looks, and she's got balls too," Alec answered with a grin. "She's got Michael's number, that's for sure."

Sebastian chuckled. "Alec, she's got all our numbers. That woman will take no shit. I kind of feel sorry and envious for any male she takes as her bonded."

Dominic didn't miss the look in his direction as this was being said.

"He will be one lucky bastard, that's for sure," Cooper piped up, and Dominic couldn't agree more. Yet the thought of her with any male made his blood boil and his fists clench. A loud knock at the door saved the men seeing how on edge he truly was. All it would take was one look in his eyes to know.

"Callum, welcome to the royal suite."

"Wow, what's that smell?" Callum, one of the alphas, chimed in as he led his bonded mate through the door.

"That, my friend, would be Cooper."

"Hey, fuck you!" Cooper piped up, and Dominic let himself smile as he watched Sebastian clip Cooper around the head.

"Language. Ladies present."

Helena laughed, the sound so welcome after seeing her so broken, before she kissed her male and moved towards the other rooms in the search of their new queen. "You boys behave."

As if timed, they all responded, "Always," followed by a laugh.

Sebastian moved to the door. "Unfortunately, Michael wasn't talking out of his arse. There really has been a new installation found. Gamma team have been debriefed."

Dominic nodded and moved, his eyes on his men. "Callum, you stay here with the females. The rest of you are with me. Let's make this quick. You know the drill. Meet in ten by the portal."

Dominic left the royal suite and hated every step away from Constance, but his job, first and foremost, was the protection of the race. And any installation that experimented on immortals needed irradiating. The other factions did their best, but the enforcers were trained for this.

Dominic just hoped they got there in time to save the souls who had been captured. He focused on what he needed to do and not on the dark-haired female who had started to haunt his dreams and every waking thought. Maybe a little destruction was just what he needed.

19

Jobs to do.

IT HAD BEEN A WEEK SINCE CONSTANCE HAD SEEN DOMINIC. A long, gruelling week of meetings, along with learning everything she could from Helena and a lovely older succubi male called Albert. Helena had stated she trusted the male with her life, and that was good enough for her. Turned out, he was also the healer.

The politics of the succubi race were was confusing as the politics in the human world, and she had never taken much notice of that. But now she had to. Albert had informed her as much, but had also said she performed well on her first day and was a natural, just like her mother. He had been the healer in charge when she had been born. The male made her feel at home immediately and made her smile.

But even with all of that happening, she still missed Dominic. Constance knew he had his own role to perform as leader of the enforcers, but she still pined for his presence. She had become more and more irritable as the week progressed. Her palm, where her new mark was, itched, but she couldn't scratch it. Every time she tried, the itch moved, and it was driving her up the wall.

As expected, Albert had performed a medical examination and answered the questions she had wanted answering since she turned eighteen. The need to have sex was from her succubi genes, and as embarrassing as it was, they had also discussed why she was unable to orgasm.

Being a succubi female meant that your first orgasm was meant to be with the male you bonded with. Now, the succubi bonded for life, so it was a big deal. Usually, for a female brought up in Helvetia, she would know her bonded from a young age. They would be drawn to each other, so by the time the female hit her maturity, love would already be there.

That's where things got heated. A female would hit her maturity around the age of eighteen, and at that time, she would need to fully bond with her male. That meant sex and blood.

Constance had been shocked to find out that it was the females who essentially ruled the race, and that it was the males' jobs to calm the females. If a female didn't bond by the time she matured, she would turn, and that there was the cause of the sex demon myths.

A turned female fed on blood, sex, and the life-force of any male she encountered, and could bring down armies if left unchecked. Such females had to be terminated.

The story gave Constance pause. She had gone through her own maturity yet had not turned. It was also the reason why she could never orgasm. Albert was unsure how she had survived, or how the males she had been with had, or why she hadn't gone feral, but she was thankful. All it did was create more questions.

Constance clutched the small envelope in her hand. She had found it the day she opened the royal suite. It was from her mother and hadn't left her person since she had first opened it. She had read it about ten times so far, but what little it did say hit her straight in the heart.

My darling daughter,

I know this letter will be one of many shocks for you. You will have a lot to learn about your role and your purpose in your new world.

When I sent you away with Gabriella, I had no choice. It broke my heart to do so, and please know that I loved you with every breath in my body. But it wasn't safe.

There are powers at work within the succubi race, ones that want an end to my reign. Your father, my bonded, was taken from us, and I fear I won't be far behind. I will join him in the afterlife, and we will both watch down on you from above.

Find my journal, my daughter, and be the leader I know you are capable of. It's in your blood.

Never forget we loved you.

Your mother.

The letter only led to, again, more questions, but did answer why her 'fake' mother had been a little bit tapped. She had been forced away from all that she knew to look after a child who wasn't hers and who would attract danger.

Constance snorted as she pocketed the letter. She didn't blame her for going loopy.

Constance sat curled up on the small sofa in front of the huge fireplace. This was her go to spot now. One where she could be warm and look up at her mum and dad. Regret that she had never known them filled her, but there was little she could do about it. In her short time as Queen so far, she had sorted through the rooms. Nothing was thrown away. Everything here had belonged to her parents and would be cherished, but they had made room for her to stamp her own mark on the place.

The gowns that had belonged to her mother, though, would be used. Each one was breath-taking, and Constance couldn't wait to wear them. She only had to wear them to go to the council chamber, which was a relief.

Corsets were not her idea of fun.

"My lady." Helena's soft voice pulled Constance from watching the flames, only to find her holding a large mug of tea.

"Thank you." She smiled and held both hands around the china. "Helena," she called out, thinking her new lady in waiting had gone, only to find she was there.

"Yes, my lady."

"Please call me Constance or Connie. If I hear 'my lady' one more time today, I may scream."

"Yes," she paused, "Connie."

"Thank you! Now, when you met Callum, how old were you?"

"I believe I knew he was mine when I was about six years old," Helena said with a smile

"That young?" Constance was stunned by how young the succubi were when they found their mates.

"Yes, but we had been around each other from, I think, two years old. I looked up to him and followed him about. It wasn't until we were in our teens did he start to admit that we were meant for each other."

"Ahh, ok." Constance took a sip of her tea. "So you claimed him first?"

Helena tilted her head and thought about it, then nodded. "Yes, I think I did."

Constance thought more. "How did you know?"

"Know what, my... Connie."

"That he was yours?" Constance asked, eager to know the signs.

"Oh." Helena blushed. "As a child, I wanted to be around him always. I felt safe and protected. But as a woman approaching my maturity..." Helena blushed more, this time going bright red, "he, in short... turned me on."

"That wasn't just it, was it?" Constance questioned, frowning.

"No, it wasn't just that. I craved seeing him. If we didn't see each other for a few days, I would find myself pining for him. His scent would drive me nuts. I would even walk past other males, but theirs did nothing for me. And my hand would itch, like my bonding mark wanted to come through but couldn't. Not yet. But mostly, I knew here." Helena placed a hand over her heart and smiled. "I knew deep in my soul and my heart he was mine."

Constance stayed quiet for a few moments, before she uncurled herself and stood. Distractedly, she placed her mug on the mantel and headed towards the front doors of the suite.

"Connie?" Helena questioned, running after her. "Is everything ok?"

Constance stopped and hugged Helena, only to giggle at the shocked look on her face when she pulled back.

"I'm fine. I've just realised I need to act like a true female succubi and go claim my male."

Helens eyes widened, and she smiled brightly. Constance gave her shoulders a quick squeeze before she moved to the door.

Alec was her guard for the day.

"My lady, where are you going?" Alec called out as she

marched past. She stopped herself from rolling her eyes at the 'my lady' part but said nothing, just kept on walking.

"My lady," he called again, and ran to catch up.

"Dominic's room. Where it is?" she asked, and stopped, facing the enforcer.

"Err, I'm sorry?" was his only response.

This time she did roll her eyes. Smirking, she watched as the male fumbled.

"Dominic's room. Which way?" she asked again, and raised an eyebrow when he didn't answer straight away. She was close to putting her hands on her hips and tapping a foot before he finally answered.

"I will take you."

"Marvellous," she replied, and grinned. It was time for the queen to claim her mate, even if he was being stubborn.

Dominic was hers. Her itchy palm confirmed it.

20

Lies and Deceit

MICHAEL TAPPED HIS FINGERS AGAINST HIS DESK. HIS EYES were glued to the wall, but they weren't looking at anything. He was deep in thought. Idea after idea flowed through his head, and all were based on one subject: power.

Or more importantly, how he would keep it. His little world where he was top dog had been overthrown. Only, it wouldn't be that way for long. No, he had plans for the new queen. Ones that involved her either disappearing or dying.

Preferably the latter.

In her first week on the job, she had thwarted his reasoning for arranged bondings, informing the race that things would go back to the way they had been when her stupid bitch of a mother had ruled. This alone had made the succubi public sit up and take notice, and of course, they loved her.

Michael clenched his fists. Of course they did. She was now an icon, a symbol of hope for a race that believed themselves to be in the dark. Michael didn't see it as being in the dark though. Nope, he was leading them to a new future. A future that would have room for the strong and pure.

He needed her gone before she thwarted any more of his plans or found out what really happened to her dear parents. Michael smiled. Now there was a thought. Picking up his phone, he dialled a number he hadn't used in years yet still knew by heart.

"Well, this is a surprise," the voice answered, although surprise didn't lace its tone. In fact, it sounded annoyed.

"I have need of you," Michael replied, trying his best to not let impatience tinge his own voice.

"Oh really? And what, pray tell, does the all-powerful leader of the succubi want?"

"I need help maintaining my leadership," Michael answered honestly. The master, as he was known to those in the underground channels, was who had carried out the plan to rid the race of the queen and her regent. It would be the master again who helped him get rid of the new queen.

"Ahh, so it's true. The rightful heir has returned." The master's voice sounded almost amused.

"This is no laughing matter," Michael snapped, his patience wearing thin.

"No, it is not. The death of a female should not be celebrated." The master's voice changed, and Michael felt a twinge of fear. "I will assist this once, but it is the last time you will call on me."

"I don't care, just get it done. I will let your men in. Just get it done with no witnesses." Michael voice shook with anger before he slammed the phone back onto the desk.

The queen would die, and he would once again be left to rule, as was his right. With her gone, he would need to put the blame on someone else, and what other way to turn the race on its head than to blame the ones they looked to for protection.

21

The Battle Within

DOMINIC WAS BONE TIRED. THE PAST WEEK, THE TEAM HAD slept little. The information Michael had provided had been spot on. The installation had been a similar set up to the one they had destroyed when the alphas had found Helena. Only this one was bigger.

The poor creatures that had been held there and tortured was staggering. The humans had managed to capture a member from nearly every race of immortals. Instead of destroying the facility this time, they had spent days digging for any information on who was behind the atrocities. Most of the captives had been too close to death to help, so they had done the most humane thing they could. Liaising with the other immortals hadn't been easy. Fights, as was the norm, broke out between certain races.

Dominic couldn't claim innocence this time though. His nerves had already been on edge, so provoking him hadn't taken much at all. Somehow, he had managed to get himself in a brawl with two fae and a were. He had held his own, his strength fuelled by a rage that had come out of nowhere. A rage that had over taken his whole body and delivered a smack down that had all the other immortal warriors retreating.

It had taken his entire alpha team to separate him from the other fighters who had been unconscious on the floor. He hadn't missed their worried looks at his battered face or his bright red eyes. Whatever his other half was, it was getting stronger, taking over until he had no control.

Getting back to the succubi mansion in Helvetia had been a must, and he had instantly secluded himself away in his quarters. But not before checking on news as to how Constance had been doing. If he was honest, being away from her for the whole week had been brutal. She never left his thoughts, and the mere mention of her name had his ears pinned back like a fucking meercat on guard. Somehow, he felt his anger stemmed from that. Being away from a female who was so out of his league, it was like a cat and a canary being together. It just didn't happen. Period.

As soon as Dominic had checked the new queen was ok, he had dived into the shower, washing away the blood from his fight. He was a quick healer—as were all the warriors—but the beat down had taken its toll. One that only rest would help solve.

He had a black eye that now looked purple, along with a split lip, His torso was a living painting of colours. Those bruises ranged from yellow to deep black, with all the rainbow mixed in. Gashes covered his back from his brief tussle with the were, but they would heal.

Standing in his bathroom, Dominic looked at his reflection in the steamy mirror. Swiping a hand across the service, his eyes, which were usually green, were now muddy, the red tinge now a permanent fixture staring back at him.

Leaning forward, he pulled his lower eyelid down to get a better look.

"What the fuck are you?" he asked his reflection. His voice echoed around him in the tiled room. Did he really expect an answer? No one knew what he was. And if shit kept moving at the speed it was, he would have to make some harsh decisions. Like leaving.

If he was a danger to his men, he would be an even bigger danger to the new queen. Although the thought of her in pain or in danger sent a wave of protectiveness through him so fierce it nearly sent him to his knees. She was his to protect, that was the vow he had made when he had discovered she was marked. Constance could never be his as a woman was to a man. The race would never allow it, even if she would. There were rules about half-breeds and purebreds. Rules that couldn't be thwarted.

What would she want with a half-breed like him anyway?

Self-destructive thoughts filled his head; not good enough, not pure enough, not man enough.

The porcelain of the sink creaked as Dominic's strength pushed against it. Only a loud knock on his door stopped its imminent destruction.

Throwing his jeans on, Dominic stalked to the door. He had told his men not to disturb him unless it was life or death. Throwing the door open, he was halted in the tirade that almost left his mouth.

"Constance," he whispered, forgetting himself. She looked amazing. Dressed for comfort, she wore jeans and a hoodie. Her hair was in a simple braid that hung over her shoulder, and her blue eyes sparkled.

"Hello, Dominic." She paused as her eyes widened. "Jesus Christ on a cracker, what the fuck happened to your face?" she blurted out. Dominic ignored her question, ignored the worried expression that flitted across her face. He ignored the bloom within his chest at her concern. Instead, he stepped out her path as she reached out to touch his face.

"My lady," Dominic said as he dropped to one knee. He had been so surprised to see her at his door, he had almost forgotten she was first and foremost his queen.

"Oh, don't you bloody start," she complained as she walked past his knelt form and into his room. "Get up, for god's sake, and close the damn door." Her voice, although annoyed, made him smile. If only for a second.

Dominic was at a loss for words. When they had first met, she hadn't been this... confident. Dominic found he liked it. A lot. Shutting the door, he leaned against it, crossing his arms as he faced her. Many a night he had fantasised about having her in his domain. He wanted it more than he realised, and for once, he found that his other half seemed calmed by her presence.

"Where have you been?" Her words were not the ones he had expected. Neither was the look of hurt that flashed across her face. "And what the hell happened to you?"

With his back already against the door, Dominic couldn't move as she approached. Before her hands could connect with his face, Dominic gripped her gently around the wrists. His heart pounded in his chest and her eyes drew him in. What was it about this woman that called to him, made his forget everything else but her?

"It's nothing, and I will heal, my lady. As to where have I been; I've been doing my job."

"It's Constance," she argued back, but didn't try to remove her hands from his. His thumb had already started to gently caress the skin of her wrist, smoothing over the pulse point and enjoying the beat of her heart. In that moment, something changed. A jolt of electricity sizzled through him, fleeting but instantaneous in its effect. Her scent filled his nostrils, which, in turn, set his body on fire. The memories of their kiss and the taste of her blood flooded his system and made maintaining control difficult.

Dominic didn't answer her as she corrected him. Instead, he released her hands and moved past her, away from the door. Away from her intense gaze and sinful lips. Away from her scent that reminded him of lilies and nights of passion.

"What can I do for you, my queen?" Dominic snapped. His fists clenched, as did his stomach, as need coursed through him. Not sensing her, Dominic jumped as she placed the flat of her hand on his back. Instantly, he moved away, and this time faced her. He didn't trust himself to revel in her touch—hell, just being in the same room was testing his control.

"Don't," he snapped again.

"Why?" she asked, but didn't move to follow him. The look of sadness on her face was nearly his undoing.

Instead of answering, he shook his head. He could never make her understand, and she could never truly want him. What she felt was most likely gratitude from her rescue. That was all it could be.

In the time it had taken Dominic to walk to the bed and pick up a shirt, Constance's demeanour had changed. Gone was the confident woman who had barged into his room, and now stood a female who cried out for comfort. The sight ripped a hole in his chest.

Tears fell from her eyes as she looked up at him, before she slowly sank to her knees. Dominic moved forward quickly. Was she ill?

"Why don't you want me?" her voice cried and stopped Dominic in his tracks. "What is wrong with me?" Stunned, Dominic was locked into place, but his gaze was drawn to her hands as they scratched at the palms.

"At my place, you wanted me—you kissed me. Yet now I'm a queen, you won't even touch me. Why?" she screamed, anger replacing the tears.

"You think I don't want you?"

"Well, duh! That's what I just said," she snapped, and pushed herself back to her feet. "Typical really. I think I've found the guy who could be it for me—that my new Spidey sense tells me could be mine—and he doesn't fucking want me."

Constance screamed in frustration and covered her face with her hands. Her voice became muffled as she continued, "My emotions are so fucking messed up. I look like a whining bitch. You've made me look like whining bitch." She screamed again, but this time her eyes pinned him with anger. He watched as Constance turned and headed for the door.

"My palms itch for you, Dominic, but you know what... fuck you." Dominic couldn't stop his jaw from sliding open at her words. He should let her go, even if her words had stopped his heart and restarted it again to beat in time with hers. Even if she had basically said she thought he was her mate. He should let her go. That would be the smart thing to do.

Dominic wasn't smart, though, was he? No, he was a dumbass—the king of.

Moving quickly, Dominic reached out and grabbed Constance's upper arm, turning her so she faced him. Her face was still wet from her tears, only now her eyes spat anger, and he welcomed it. His other half burned inside, urging him to claim her, make her finally his.

"You think it's that fucking easy?" he spat out, his fingers gripping harder as he moved them to her shoulders and shook her a little. Hoping she would see sense.

"I can't want you, Constance—fuck, I'm not allowed to want you," Dominic shouted back, and was rewarded as her eyes widened. His right hand left her shoulder and moved slowly up her throat, past the small scarred puncture marks from her attack. His thumb caressed the skin there before his hand reached her face. He cupped her cheek gently.

"There are rules, sweetheart, ones that even you, as the queen, should follow." His voice softened only a touch.

"I can't want you, Constance," he repeated, "but I do. Everything about you calls to me like a fucking siren."

"W—what?" Constance stuttered, and Dominic saw the pulse in her neck jump.

"Don't you get it? Everything about you drives me crazy; your scent, your eyes, your lips." He listed everything he loved about her. "You have an arse that drives me nuts, and all I want to do, all I've ever fantasised about since meeting you, is getting so deep within you, you no longer know where you end or I begin."

He paused, loving the way her eyes darkened with desire at his words, but also knowing his next words would destroy that look.

"But I can't. I have my honour and word as an alpha, and that is more important."

If he could have kicked himself for the hurt he put on her face, he would have. Hell, Dominic would have beaten himself to a pulp for it. What was he supposed to do, give in to lust and desire with no regards to his race?

The enforcers looked to him to set an example, and what

kind of one would he be setting if he let his sexual desires dictate his actions. Dominic's heart clenched as he watched the desire bleed from Constance's face, quickly replaced by seething rage.

"You know what?" she said angrily through clenched teeth. Instead of continuing her sentence, she held up both hands and gave him the middle fingers, followed by a growl. In any other circumstance, it would be funny, even cute, but even Dominic didn't have the balls to say that out loud.

He watched as she stood there, before she shook her still held up middle fingers and then turned. Throwing open the door to his room, she screamed in frustration as she slammed it.

Yes, he was a dumbass. Letting her go had been for the best, yet... why did it hurt like hell?

∽

That man drove her nuts and then some.

"ARSEHOLE," she squealed through clenched teeth as she slammed the door to his room and stood in the corridor. Rage and pent-up desire warred for dominance inside her.

Dammit, why was he being so unreasonable? They wanted each other, so why was he being a twunt about it? Yes, a twunt. She nodded internally. A male who's a cross between a twat and a cunt. Constance snorted but still didn't move from in front of his door. She hoped he would follow her out.

The romantic inside of her hoped he would waltz out and take her in his arms, declaring his undying love. She paused. Yeah, that wasn't going to happen, was it. This wasn't some fairy tale; it was real life, which meant, for Constance, happy endings didn't happen.

"My lady," a deep voice called out, and Constance turned. Pleased to see a familiar face, she tried to smile.

"Sebastian." Constance wanted to force being cheerful but couldn't muster the strength.

"What is wrong?" the tall male asked. He was handsome —hell, all the alpha team were in their own ways and wouldn't struggle to get a lady to drop her panties for them. Yet there was only one who could do that for her and he was being an arse.

"How long have you got?" she replied as she looked at Dominic's door, before she forced another smile.

She heard Sebastian sigh, then watched as he held out his arm for her and waited. She hated feeling like this— wanted something to take the pain away. Sliding her arm into the crook of his, she let him pull her along, only it wasn't back towards her royal suite.

"Where are we going?" she asked, a little nervous. She hadn't been let out of the royal suite or the council chambers since she had arrived. This was all new territory.

"To give you a break and show you that this place isn't all meetings and politics." He smiled brightly, and Constance couldn't help but return one of her own. She fought the need to look back at Dominic's door, fought it and won.

That male would not be the boss of her or her emotions. That's what she had to keep telling herself anyway.

22

———

Enforcers

SEBASTIAN HAD MANAGED IN ONLY A SHORT TIME TO MAKE HER feel at home and not the outcast she had always felt. Even when they had brought her back, she had felt like she didn't belong. Placed up high on a pedestal as Queen, untouchable and not worthy of friendship.

Sebastian had walked her into the enforcers common area as if she belonged there, and every single male had dropped to their knees. Fists over their chests, it had been a humbling sight. But she didn't want everyone to kneel every time she walked into a room. So she had broken the ice by politely telling them to "get the fuck up".

Constance had been pleased when the males had all laughed and did as she had asked. Her evening had gone from crappy to actually not too bad, although Dominic still remained on her mind.

"My lady, it's your turn."

Pulled from her thoughts of Mr. Green-eyed and Sexy, she eyed her opponent.

"I told you, Bash, it's Connie or nothing." She mock growled as she bent over the snooker table and fired the white ball into a red. She grinned when it slid easily into the pocket, giving her another shot.

"Bash, are you getting your arse whooped by a—" The comment stopped and Constance couldn't help but laugh.

"Please, go on." She smirked and turned to the owner of the voice. He didn't. "Billy, wasn't it?" She waited until he nodded, looking less like the strong enforcer and more like a child about to get told off.

"Billy, if you were going to say, by a girl—which I hope you weren't—I hope you have the man-plums to back yourself up, 'cause, sweetheart," she paused and pointed her cue, " when I'm done with your buddy here, you are next."

With that, Constance turned and fired the white again, loving the groan of disappointment when she sunk another red.

Finally, she started to feel like she belonged. She loved the banter, because she knew that was all it was. If it came down to it, these males would do their best to protect her from harm.

That right there meant more than any of them could ever know.

Bending over the table again, Constance was about to aim when she heard, then felt, a large hand slap her arse. Hard. For a second, she had hoped it was Dominic, yet she knew instantly he would never cause her harm, and he wouldn't dare do something like that in public. Constance raised her eyes and looked at the enforcers. Each had stood and eyed the culprit with hatred. Slowly, she turned.

"Well, my lady, what a fine arse you have—and it felt good, too." The male was tall, similar in height to Bash, who had now rounded the table and stood to her right.

"My arse is off limits to you, enforcer. Was there a reason you touched it?" She sneered. She knew who the male was. Helena had pointed him out to her as one of Michael's chosen few. Shane. She'd deliberately used his role instead of his name. He had overstepped the mark by touching her, yet he didn't care. That was worrying in itself.

"But it begged to be touched." He leered at her. "Much like the rest of you."

His look made her skin crawl and made the enforcers growl. She watched as Sebastian stepped forward.

"Shane," he started, his tone full of warning.

"Shut up, Sebastian. I'm not afraid of you or the alphas. You are all obsolete in the eyes of our leader."

Constance had known there was friction within the enforcer ranks, but seeing it up close made her wonder what Michael had done to garner such loyalty. She also knew they hadn't dared fight due to the backlash that Michael could and would deliver. He had the enforcers on a tight leash.

"Shane, back the fuck off before we make you." Bash moved forward, placing Constance behind him. She felt grateful, but she could feel her own anger building.

"Now wait a minute. By leader, you are referring to Michael?" She stepped around Bash, placing her hand on his arm to show him she was ok.

"Sorry, but, you know, I'm new here, and forgive me if I'm wrong..." she paused and smiled at the enforcers who had her back before she looked up at Shane, "I thought I was your leader. You know, being Queen and all that jazz."

Constance raised an eyebrow and watched Shane. The sweat on his brow showed he wasn't the big bollocky Bill he thought he was.

"You have no idea what you are messing with... Your

Highness." Shane sneered and bent his head, bringing it closer to her own. The smell of his breath made her stomach churn. The male had never met a toothbrush in his life, she was certain. She shuddered.

Before Bash or Sebastian could stop him, he reached out and grabbed her, pulling her body to his as he smashed his lips against her own. Constance squealed, lifting her hands to claw at his face even as the room erupted around her. Enforcers moved forward en masse, even though they couldn't do anything without risking her safety. Shane had pulled one over on all of them.

Constance felt tears fill her eyes as Shane became brutal in the kiss, trying to force her mouth open. Bile rose, and she couldn't stop the whimper of distress that left her. Buzzing filled her ears, joined by a loud roar.

She felt herself being ripped from Shane's arms and pressed against the solid chest of another. She recognised his scent immediately.

Dominic.

23

Taking Control

Dominic had paced his room continuously, the inner debate still unsolved, and he felt like a whiny child because of it. He was a grown male. He led others. Surely he should be able to make a damn decision.

She wanted him—she had made that clear—and what had he done? Told her no. Why? Because he thought honour and his word meant more. They had, at one point, but as soon as he had seen her that night in the bar, his thoughts had been filled with her. Even when he had thought her human.

She wanted him.

That one thought circled his brain.

She wanted him.

She didn't care that he was a half-breed. Didn't care that he wasn't a pureblood. Constance didn't care about any of the things that had set him apart from everyone else for all his life.

She wanted him.

Dominic looked at the door. She wanted him and, dammit, he wanted her with every fibre of his being. As if on cue, a knock sounded at his door. Moving quickly, he threw it open, Constance's name on his lips.

"Con—Callum?"

"Dom, you need to get to the common room," Callum blurted out, his chest heaving from running.

"Why, what's going on?" He frowned. Callum was usually the calm one.

"Constance is there. Shane is causing a scene… again."

Dominic growled, a now all too common sound from him. "What?"

"He…err… He touched her, and that's when I came for you. She had the rest of the enforcers there, but you know Shane."

"Let's go," was all Dominic said as he slammed his door. He still hadn't put a shirt on but that was the last thing on his mind. His thoughts centred around Shane and the fact he had put his hands on his female.

Yeah, she was his.

It took moments for them to reach the common area. What he saw made him see red.

Shane had Constance in his arms and was kissing her, even as she fought to get away. The enforcers were poised ready, but they couldn't risk hurting Constance, and they were also at risk of Michael's punishment should they hurt Shane, who had become Michael's fuck boy.

Dominic didn't care. This male was overstepping one big, monumental fucking line.

In two steps, he was next to Shane. Grabbing the back of the male's neck, he squeezed hard enough to hear the crunch of bone grating against bone, followed by his bellow of pain. As soon as the male had released his lip-lock on Constance, he had her in his arms.

"You dare touch our queen?" Dominic's voice thundered within the room.

He watched as Shane caught his breath as he held the back of his neck. He glared at Dominic.

"Why not? You seem to be ok touching her," the male argued back. But before he had chance to reply, Constance piped up, her anger making her shake.

"You!" she shouted and twisted in his arms. "You are never to come anywhere near me again. You are unworthy of being an enforcer." Her voice wavered, but only slightly. She looked at Dominic. From her position in his arms, she was eye to eye. Right now, her eyes pleaded.

"I don't want him near me."

Dominic nodded and felt his anger rising again as he looked at her bruised lips and unshed tears.

"Sebastian, remove Shane. In fact, throw him in the cells."

"What? You can't do that! Michael will have something to say."

"I'm sure he will, but I couldn't give a toss. You have violated one of our oaths; placing our charge, our queen, in danger. Danger from yourself. You are unworthy of being an enforcer," Dominic spat out, and then turned with Constance in his arms.

"You will pay for this. You and your little bitch." Shane's words were followed by a cry of pain. Dominic didn't see the dull thwack as a fist made contact. He heard shouts as he left the common area with his queen in his arms. Her giggle made him pause.

"Constance?" he questioned, unsure for the reason of her giggle. Could it be hysterics? Still she didn't answer.

Dominic had moved further down the corridor, wanting to get her as far away as possible from Shane. Sliding her down his body, he turned her to face him. Her face was red, her eyes glistened, and her lips were swollen, yet she took his breath away with her smile.

"Sorry," she finally answered him. "Billy punched him." She giggled. "Like full on throat punched him, and then gave me a thumbs up." He watched as she wiped her eyes and laughed again. "I couldn't stop the giggle."

Dominic nodded, and without thinking, reached up to move a strand of hair from her face, letting his fingers caress the skin of her cheek. She paused, her eyes wide as she watched him.

"Are you ok?" his voice croaked. "Did he hurt you?" Dominic had fought so hard to stop himself from ripping Shane apart, his main aim to get Constance out of the male's arms. Seeing her with another male, even unwillingly, had made him see there was no fighting what he felt for this woman. He didn't want to fight anymore.

"Yes. I'm alright, thank you," she answered. He watched her eyes move from his face to his chest. Seconds passed by as emotion after emotion flashed across her face. When it settled, Dominic felt his stomach drop. Rage. Eyebrows drawn together, she lifted her gaze to his before she thumped him hard in the chest.

"You are such a bellend." Her voice was quiet, but every word was pronounced. "You... you..." She paused as if trying to find the right word, only Dominic wouldn't let her say it.

Bending his head, he took her mouth, moving his lips against hers, coaxing her to open, wanting to erase what Shane had done and mark her himself. Dominic smirked as she sighed then opened to him, her tongue meeting his.

She was perfection. She was *his*.

Wrapping his arms around her, Dominic lifted her and turned. He walked and kissed—a challenge in itself, but it was needs must when it came to his female.

And he wanted her in his room, in his bed, as soon as possible.

Dominic revelled in the feel of her hands that had now buried themselves in his hair. Loved the feel of her against his body. Her lush softness to his hardness.

She was quickly becoming his obsession and he loved it.

As he finally made it to his door, he pushed through the portal and slammed it behind him. Dominic moved to the centre of the room and let her, again, slide down his body.

Constance's eyes were no longer filled with anger or hurt. Dominic didn't fight the smirk that crossed his lips. Her eyes now reflected back his own lusts and desires, and didn't that just boost his ego and need.

His cock felt like a lead weight against the fly of his jeans as most of his blood pooled south. She may be a queen—his queen—but in his room, he was in charge.

Cupping the back of her head, Dominic leaned forward. "Say no now, Constance, because when I start, there's no stopping. Rules or not, I will make you mine," Dominic stated out loud. The turmoil he had felt now vanished, leaving behind only resolve. He would deal with the consequences later. The woman in his arms right now was all that mattered to him.

"You want this? You want me?" he asked, and held his breath as he waited for an answer.

"I want you, Dom," she breathed out, and then bit her lip. Her hands had moved up and now rested against his bare chest. Her touch was like a match, setting his blood on fire. In that moment, nothing else mattered but her.

"You got me," he answered, before he slanted his mouth

over hers and took control. He moved his hands from her face, down past her curves, to cup her delicious arse. In one move, he lifted her and stalked forward, pinning her against the wall as he possessed her mouth like a man dying of thirst and finding she was his oasis. Her moans filled the air and urged him on.

Dominic would never be the same again after this. Neither would she. He would make damn well sure of it.

24

This Kiss

DOMINIC'S KISS WAS EVERYTHING SHE HAD IMAGINED AND more. Heat flowed through her as if her blood was liquid magma, and she revelled in it. Before, when she had been with a man, she had taken control to try and get what she needed. Only now, she gave that control up freely. Dominic had stated confidently in her flat that he could give her what she craved, and she believed him.

When Alec had shown her to Dominic's room, she had been concerned, seeing a lot of the warriors all bore injuries. Fear that Dominic had been hurt had her almost running to the door. She had dismissed Alec and had stood confidently, waiting for Dominic to answer the door. Only he had ruined everything by denying her.

What had just happened in the common room though... As much as it had scared her, it had done something to Dominic, getting him to see her as not just the queen but a woman in need of her man as well. Something had changed in his eyes, and she had revelled in it. Only now, she was distracted again. Dominic still hadn't put a shirt on, and she would prefer that to be the norm.

Only, she hadn't been prepared for two things. One: the concern she had felt when she had seen his bruises and other injuries earlier, and two: the way her body had reacted to a half-naked Dominic.

Drool had threatened to drip from her wide-open mouth at the sight of defined muscle, and there was a lot of it. Constance had known Dominic was no pigeon-chested tosser. She had got a good feel of his pecs when she had been resting her head against them as he had carried her home. But now, with nothing covering them, she was spellbound.

Muscles had always done it for her; a sign of hard work and strength. Dominic's chest was huge, with pecs that could easily spend the rest of their lives as her personal pillow. But it wasn't just the pecs that had caused Constance to barely be able to contain herself. She had wanted to sigh and purr at the same time as her gaze had wandered down its own yellow brick road, or in this case, a golden, tanned brick road of ripped abdominal muscles leading to every girl's happy place. The way to heaven.

Constance had ripped her eyes away and tried to act all queen like. Luckily for her, Dominic had dropped to his knee and saved her a shit load of embarrassment. It had taken everything she had to walk past, only to be distracted by his taut biceps and back muscles.

Constance was a perv—that she knew already—but she hadn't been aware of the level, until now. Yes, she was a class ten with golden stars. As she had looked around the room, she tried her best to get her thoughts into line. She had tried to remember why she was there... Oh yes, he made her palms itch.

That's when her emotions had gotten the better of her and she had screamed like a crazy lady. Well, that was what happened when you were denied an orgasm for a long period of time. What she hadn't expected was Dominic's own reaction, or his words.

But the outcome had been what she had wanted; his hands on her and their tongues duelling for dominance. She wanted this more than she wanted her next breath. Since the moment she had seen him in the bar, he had never left her thoughts or her fantasies.

Pulling her mouth away from his, Constance panted as her thighs tightened around his waist.

"Dom... please," was all she could manage before she licked her lips and pressed them back to his.

A new flavour came into play, sending what little brain function she had retained south, along with all the blood as her core tingled in response. The copper tang gave way to a mixture of cinnamon and hot chocolate. Constance had felt lust before—hell, her whole life had been dictated by it— but this was something different. Something inside clicked as the new taste coated her tongue.

Dominic's blood.

She was doing something she had never thought she would be capable of: she was feeding. In the aggressiveness of their kiss, the cut he had on his lip had opened, giving Constance her first feed as a succubi female.

"Oh god," she screamed, "you taste so good." Constance's hands gripped his head and held him to her. All the while, he moaned and thrust his hard arousal against her jean-covered core. Her body revelled in each new sensation as she skyrocketed closer to an orgasm than she ever had before. Sucking hard on Dominic's lip, Constance then threw her head back and screamed. Her body erupting over and over.

"Fucking hell... so damn sexy." Dominic's hoarse words filtered in through her ears and she looked down at the man who had given her what no other could. Blood coated one side of his face, but it was his eyes that made her gasp, even as he kept up the gentle thrusting, his body still rock hard.

"Better?" he croaked out, and all Constance could do was nod.

"Good. Now it's time to have the real fun." Constance's body clenched in need as he pulled her from the wall and walked her over to the bed. Bending, Dominic placed her on top of the covers and gently untangled her legs from around his waist.

"This time, my queen, I am going to take my sweet time with you." His words were confidently spoken. Constance watched as he slowly undressed her, his fingers caressing her skin as it was revealed.

"What's my name?" Constance shivered as Dominic stretched out beside her and whispered in her ear.

"What's my name, Constance?" he asked again, and Constance could only whisper her answer.

"Dominic."

"Good." She watched as he grinned and bent his head, licking a path down her throat to her now bare chest. Both nipples pebbled in the cool air, begging for his touch.

"Good?" she questioned, although rational thought was no longer possible.

"Yes, good," he answered as he blew hot air across her left nipple, making her gasp. "I'm just checking you know exactly what to scream when I make you come." Thought completely fled as he latched his wicked lips around the erect peak and sucked.

"Oh god, I'm going to die," she moaned aloud as her hands once again went to Dominic's hair. His chuckle vibrated against her skin, making her stomach clench.

"Never, my queen." His voice sounded close again, and Constance opened her eyes to find Dominic watching her, his face mere inches from her own as his hand slowly made its way towards her core. Her eyes never left his as he made contact, sweeping a large digit across her entrance and making her hiss in pleasure.

"Fuck! So wet..." He smirked, knowing it was his doing.

"Are you ready, my queen?" he asked as he leaned on his elbows, placing his body in the cradle of her own. His right hand cupped her cheek, whilst the other one positioned his hard cock at her entrance then lifted her leg, again wrapping it around his waist.

Constance was lost, lost to feeling and to her emotions. Looking into Dominic's eyes, she finally felt a sense of belonging. This enforcer had wormed his way, unknowingly, into her heart, and as he pressed inside her, she felt whole. Like her soul had finally found its other half.

"Oh god!" she screamed as his length filled her, his girth bigger than any of the human males she had been with. Pleasure collided with pain. His groan followed her scream as he buried his head in the crook of her neck, his lips sliding against her flesh, kissing and licking.

For a moment—a brief one—Constance remembered the painful bite of the vampyres, but the memory vanished as Dominic powered into her. She felt the slide of fangs against her skin and tilted her head to accept them. This was no vampyre. This was Dominic, and she wanted his bite.

"Do it," she begged as shivers travelled down her spine in anticipation. Dominic didn't hesitate, striking quickly.

Constance's reaction was instantaneous. Her orgasm hit so hard darkness threatened to take over. Only Dominic's rhythmic thrusting kept her grounded.

"Oh my god," she gasped again as she felt his tongue sweep up her neck, sealing the wounds.

"Not god. Dominic." His all too male chuckle filled her ears as he continued to move, each thrust taking every thought and turning it into sensation and the feel of Dominic.

Her enforcer.

Her mate.

25

Pleas of Mercy

COOPER CUPPED THE BACK OF HIS NECK AND PRESSED DOWN IN an attempt to ease the soreness that had started to set in. Why he had volunteered to help with the clean-up of their most recent mission was a mystery to himself. That being said, he would always do what his leader or queen told him to. Within reason.

Maybe this was his limit. He had never been a fan of paperwork, never mind trolling through countless pages in an attempt to find out who the ones responsible for the kidnappings and experiments were. Someone higher up the food chain was funding the operation, someone who didn't care that they were destroying lives.

Page after page revealed nothing that was of use, only what they had found out from the different immortals they had experimented on. Out of the fifteen only three had been saveable.

A fae male, a succubi male, and a female—only they didn't know what she was. She had yet to regain consciousness and, as such, was today being transferred to the succubi realm for medical help and observation. Once they had an idea of who and what she was, they would contact her race accordingly. The fae race had promised to help the succubi and their new queen in tracking down those responsible. Having them as allies was a positive step in the right direction, even if it was the only positive out of the whole cluster fuck of a situation.

Standing, Cooper moved from behind the desk and out of the cramped office. The smell of burning and antiseptic was almost stifling. It was so thick in the air it made his skin itch.

He had left Alec and Stefan to finish off destroying anything that wasn't of use, and by the smell of things, they were having far too much fun. The facility itself was a simple layout, with one long corridor with doors off to the side every four metres. Two were what he could call operating theatres, but ones that dated back to the turn of the century. Cleanliness or infection control was not something these monsters worried about. Behind other doors lay the office he had come from, a tea room, and then the holding cells.

Each cell was only four-foot squared, and there were no toilet facilities. As far as these went, they were an upgrade from what Helena, Callum's female, had been subjected to. But it was still barbaric. Cooper clenched his fists and enjoyed the cracking sound as it echoed up the empty hallway.

A scream answered him and had him moving quickly down the corridor and through the door to the holding cells. They had yet to move the female, leaving her within until it was time to leave. Only now she was awake. And pissed.

"Whoa there, calm down," Cooper called out as he watched the female run at the bars, throwing her whole body at them. Her eyes held nothing but pure fear and panic, which caused an instant response of protectiveness from Cooper.

"Come on, darling, you have to stop that before you hurt yourself." He moved towards the cell and opened the door. They had left it unlocked, a fact the female had missed in her blind panic. Opening the door, Cooper waited near the entrance.

Her eyes, a dark hazel, locked onto him. They flicked to the now open door and back to him. Cooper held his hands out to show he meant no harm, and stepped back.

"Come on, darling. Come out of the cage and let's get you sorted," Cooper cooed, but was rewarded with a hiss. Long fangs erupted from the female and they pressed down against her lower lip. Her red hair hung around her, the locks knotted and lank from lack of washing, yet even through all this and the dirt that coated her face—even though she was dressed in a hospital smock—she was hauntingly beautiful.

Cooper looked his fill as she did the same to him. Silence passed between them, as if they both waited for something. Only to have Alec break it.

"Hey, what's all the noise?"

A scream again rent the air as the female bolted for the cell door, for Cooper. Her hands outstretched, tiny claws tipped each finger as they head for his neck. Reaching up, Cooper clasped her wrists within his hands, but her momentum sent them both to the floor. Rolling them over, Cooper pinned her beneath him, using his larger body to subdue her own.

"Calm down, female. We mean you no harm," he

shouted, trying to be heard over the screaming. "Fuck! Alec, get something to calm her down before she hurts herself further."

He called over to his fellow alpha, only to see Stefan already on his way with a syringe in his hand. As gently has possible, Cooper stretched her arms over her head. Pinning her wrists in one hand, he smoothed the hair from her face. Clear tear marks could be seen, tracking their way through the dirt on her face. Her hazel eyes, although filled with fear, begged him for something. He had no idea what.

"Shhhh, it's ok." Cooper tried to calm her as Stefan bent down, and with a skill that had Cooper looking at his friend in surprise, he slid the needle into the female's arm. Within seconds, the sedative was working, her body stilling beneath his.

Her eyes, moments before they closed, released another tear that went straight to Cooper's gut, clenching it. Guilt threatened to overtake him. A sob left her lips, followed by words Cooper would never forget.

"Please... kill me."

26

The Afterglow

CONSTANCE WOKE WITH A START. HER HEARTBEAT HAMMERED against her ribcage as she sat up. She didn't recognise the room. Her stomach clenched. Had she slept with another random stranger again, in the hopes they could quench her need?

Speaking of which... She felt totally sated. Her body, instead of being on edge, now thrummed with contentment. In short, she felt good—really good. Constance smiled as finally her brain caught up with the events of the past week. Her smile got bigger, and she finally looked to her left and saw the cause of her current feelings of elation.

Dominic slept by her side, his large body taking up most of the bed. On his back, with his right arm above his head. Even in sleep he radiated power and strength. Constance was helpless to stop herself from running her palm up his broad chest. Touching him was her new favourite thing to do, and she had done plenty of that the night before. So had he, and she had revelled in every sensation he had created within her. Dominic had ruined her for all other men, that was for sure.

"Morning." His deep, sleepy voice pulled her from her thoughts, and her eyes met his green ones. The red tinge she had seen before had faded. Curiosity made her want to question what it was, but she didn't want to ruin the moment with him.

Scooting down, Constance wrapped her arm over his waist and rested her head upon his broad chest, letting her ear sit right over his heart. She felt his arm come up around her shoulders as he pulled her tighter against him. Silence reined, neither one wanting to break it, feeling like, if they did, the perfect bubble where it was just them alone would break. Only, it took a loud knock at the door to do just that.

After a minute, the knock came again, this time louder and more insistent. Reluctantly, Constance felt Dominic move. His loud sigh made her smile. Squeezing her one last time, he slid from her side. Once out of bed, he turned and looked down at her. A small smile on his own lips, he ignored the now constant knocking and bent to kiss her. Constance couldn't help the sigh that left her at the contact. She was addicted to this male. As he moved back, he pulled the covers up to her chin and tucked her in.

"I don't need tucking in, Dom." Her voice held a husky note from her night of screaming.

"I know, but I don't want whoever it is behind that door to see what's mine."

"Oh really?"

"Yes, really. I told you, sweetheart... You. Are. Mine."

With that said, he turned and slipped on his jeans—no underwear. And didn't that just make Constance's body rev up again. Her eyes took in everything, memorising each muscle. She wanted to touch them.

She had never had the opportunity in the past to watch a man dress, seeing as she skipped out as soon as she woke. But this was now something she would never miss. Dammit, she had it bad. Even his bare feet were sexy.

"I would cut that out." His voice pulled her gaze from her slow perusal of his body and up to his eyes that blazed with desire.

Constance said nothing, instead choosing to smile and then bite her lip. The small action had the desired effect, making Dominic growl deep in his throat. A sound that had her instantly wet and wanting.

Shaking his head, Dominic turned and opened the door to his room.

"What!" he snapped. Constance was unable to hear what was being said, their voices muffled.

"Fine," she heard him snap again. He shut the door. His face was a blank mask as he turned to her. Instead of re-joining her on the bed, he finished dressing.

"What's wrong?" Constance asked, only to get silence in return. That annoyed her.

"Hey! What's wrong?" she said a little louder as she climbed from beneath the duvet and started to dress herself.

"Nothing that concerns you," he replied, and Constance felt her hackles rise. Wasn't she Queen? So technically that meant everything concerned her. Especially things that put her enforcers into pissy moods.

"Right, so, as the queen, I don't get told shit, then," she snapped back as she pulled her bra on and then her top and hoodie. She looked a mess, her hair looking like she used it as a mop.

"Constance." Dominic's voice was more of a warning. "I've got to go. I've been summoned by the council."

Instead of answering, Constance folded her arms across

her chest. Why she felt she needed to know was a mystery, but she wanted to be in control, and not knowing stuff drove her wild. She watched as he walked over. Lifting his hand, he cupped her cheek.

"Stay here and wait for me?" he asked. To her, though, it felt like more of an order. "And don't tell anyone about this —about us."

"Why the hell not?" Constance felt her eyes go wide. Was he ashamed of what they had done?

"I can't explain now, there's no time. But just stay here. I will be back as soon as I can."

Constance felt the frown as it formed on her head, yet she didn't answer. Constance felt so confused, so out of her depth. She had thought claiming Dominic would help her, not just with her body's needs but with feeling like she belonged. Only, she felt she was the only one in the dark.

His lips on hers caused the answering tingles to start within her stomach, yet she fought it, refusing to close her eyes as he took control of her mouth. Trying to remain stoic was the hardest thing she had ever done. As he pulled back, his eyes, now back to their usual bright green, were full of questions.

"You had better go," she said simply, and stepped back. With a sigh that filled the room, Dominic nodded and moved to the door.

"Stay here. I won't be long." With that, Constance watched him leave. They hadn't rowed. All he had done was not tell her why he had been summoned. Why did it feel like a betrayal? Constance felt even more lost than she did before.

Constance waited ten minutes before she collected her trainers and moved to the door. She couldn't wait in his room. Not when everything reminded her of what they had done all night. He had given her relief for the first time in her life, yet she felt like that would be the only time.

Shaking her head, she left his room. Her heart ached, and her palms tingled. Looking down, Constance saw the faint outlines of her new bonding marks. She had been right; he was her mate. But she had never felt more alone than she did now.

27

To Protect or to Fail

DOMINIC'S MOOD HAD GONE FROM GOOD TO BAD FASTER THAN a Formula One car. As soon as he had closed the door to his room, he had been pissed. His night had been, in short, perfection. Lost in the arms of Constance, he had forgotten about everything that wasn't in that room with them. He had even forgotten his duty as an enforcer, never mind being the leader.

But... he couldn't muster one single feeling of guilt. That was how perfect it had felt to have her in his arms. As much as he had denied it, there was something far too powerful for them to resist, which pulled them closer. Fate had never been his friend, yet he was starting to believe that fate was playing a part now. Only, if that was true, it could have least of left him to enjoy a morning with Constance.

Even as he marched down the corridor behind Alec, knowing he had a job to do, everything in him begged him to turn around and go back. Constance had quickly taken over every though in his head. After their night, there would be no going back. Regardless of what the council said or thought, he would not give her up. Yes, she was the queen, but who better to protect her than the leader of the enforcers.

There would be the issue of his heritage, but the way he saw it, if Constance didn't care, neither should the council. It was a bridge they would have to cross, but first, he had to deal with the emergency that had Stefan banging at his door. The giant of a male was not one for many words and had simply stated that Sebastian had sent him to fetch him.

Dominic clenched his fists then unclenched them, ignoring the itch that had briefly flew across his palm. He felt irritable and on edge, and had felt that way since he had left his room. He just hoped whatever his second in command wanted was quick to deal with. He hadn't wanted to leave Constance, and his other side had only let him leave if he knew she would stay. She was his to protect.

Simply put, she was his—had been since the moment he had first seen her. It had just taken a while for his brain to catch up with his instincts.

Their booted feet echoed along the corridor as they walked through the enforcers' wing. Most of the enforcers would be training, so the corridors were empty. Stefan remained quiet as he moved aside and let Dominic lead them into the alphas' main office.

"Sebastian," he said sharply. His second in command and Alec were bent over a screen, frowns on their faces.

"What's the problem?" Dominic asked, and walked around to see what had them troubled. The screen showed multiple camera views from the surveillance they had installed. Most of the black and grey videos showed nothing, until Sebastian's hand shot out and pointed to one on the bottom left.

"Fuck! There, pause that," he shouted.

Alex, who had become a bit of a geek with the cameras, quickly rewound the footage and played it back in slow motion. All the enforcers became still as three males came into view. All dressed in black. But it was their fangs they couldn't hide. White and gleaming in the darkness.

"Fuck, we have vamps. How did they get through our portal?"

"Doesn't matter how. Where are they?" Dominic ordered, already knowing Stefan was pulling weapons free and Sebastian had simply removed his jacket. His second had a thing about using his fists.

"Royal wing. Dom..." Alec called out, concern in his voice.

"What?" Dominic answered as he pulled out his daggers.

"Our queen... she's on her way there now." Alec's voice was filled with worry.

"What!" Dominic dived around the table and watched the camera. Constance was, in fact, stomping her way down the corridor towards her own room. If it had been any other situation, Dominic would have laughed. Her arms gestured wildly as she literally stomped instead of walked away from his room. Away from safety and straight into trouble.

"Move out," Dominic ordered again. Only Alec stayed, monitoring the situation from the cameras. How vampyres had gotten into their realm he didn't know. What they wanted, though, he could guess.

They wanted his female.

～

Constance stomped hard, only her trainer clad feet made no sound on the carpeted corridor. They would have if she had stayed in the enforcers' wing. With their stone flooring, she could have made lots of noise to signal how pissed she was.

Being ordered to stay in a room that wasn't hers wasn't all she was mad about. She was mad that he had been so quick to leave her after what they had done the night before. Along with the whole "don't tell anyone", which really pissed on her orgasmic bonfire.

What a way to ruin the mood. Well, Mr. Tall, Dark and Hung... He may have floated her boat all night long, but he sure as hell wasn't going be sailing without some serious grovelling. It was amazing really—how one male could get under her skin so quickly. Yet, when she thought about it, he had burrowed his way there the first time she had perved at him in the bar. He was her type through and through. And again, if she was honest, all it would take was one look from his mesmerizing eyes and a crook of his finger and she would be at his mercy.

"Ugh, I'm so easy," Constance commented out loud as she stopped at a t-junction. This was the hard part about her new home. It was like a bloody rabbit warren.

"Which way, which way... You would think there would be bloody directions or a sign post. You know, anything," she grumbled as she looked each way. "You know, *castle this way*, or at least a worm that could show me the way."

Every corridor looked the same in this part of the mansion, and she had no clue where she was going. The corridors were eerily quiet, making the hair on the back of her neck tingle and rise.

"Female," a deep voice called from behind her, making Constance gasp as she turned. The owner of the voice was a male dressed in black.

"Oh, thank god. Can you point me in the direction of the royal wing please? I'm a little lost," she asked, but all she got in reply was snarl. His mouth opened, revealing bright white fangs.

"Err, who are you?" she asked, worry lacing her words as she stumbled backwards into the arms of another male. His arms slipped around her body, pinning her own to the side.

"Hey, get off me! Who the fuck are you?" she cried out, and started to struggle, only to have the male tighten his grasp.

"Be quiet," he snarled into her ear.

"Be gentle with her." A third male stepped into view and eyed Constance. She hated the way his eyes looked her up and down before he licked his lips. Stepping forward, he pulled a cloth from his pocket.

"What the fuck?" Constance called out, and started to struggle again, her mind a whir. These were vampyres, just like the ones that had attacked her before. Only this time, Dominic wasn't going to just rock up and save her.

She had to stall. Maybe someone would hear her if she called out. Anything. Her eyes followed the hand that held the white cloth. She knew what that was, and it wasn't good.

"Chloroform! Really?" she taunted. "Well, aren't you original," She knew it was probably a mistake, but she needed to delay them. She was fucked if he got that cloth over her face.

Constance lifted her leg and stomped her right foot down onto her captor's instep, and at the same time, fired her head upwards and backwards. She felt victorious as she heard the crunch of bone and felt her captor release her. His howl of pain gave Constance a moment of triumph, until a steel hand wrapped around her arm like a vice.

Her eyes widened slightly as she watched, in almost slow motion, as a fist came directly at her face.

The impact did its job, sending her into darkness instantly.

No pain... just darkness.

_____

28

Anger. Let it out

DOMINIC RAN THROUGH THE CORRIDORS OF HIS HOME, THE one place he had thought they would all be beyond the reach of other immortals, especially since every race had signed a truce. Helvetia was a sanctuary, but now the vamps had broken it. His brothers kept pace behind him and he was grateful. He would need their support, especially if anything had happened to Constance.

Turning down another corridor, Dominic spotted the three vampyres that had trespassed. All three turned, hissing as they spotted the enforcers with weapons drawn. Dominic ignored them, his gaze zeroing on the vamp at the back of the pack and the cargo he had thrown over his shoulder.

Constance's dark fair fell in waves and covered her head. Her arms hung limply. The bastards had knocked her out. Dominic felt something inside him swell, his other side pushing to take over. He pushed it back, needing logic if he wanted to get his female back.

"I suggest you put the female down and back the fuck away," Dominic snarled, yet all three vampyres ignored his words and turned their backs.

"Well, that's fucking rude," Cooper shouted.

Dominic said nothing. Instead, he launched himself onto the back of the vampyre nearest to him. Wrapping his arms around its neck he held on as it bucked and clawed at him. The other enforcers attacked another, knowing not to get in Dominic's way.

"I suggest you stop," the third vampyre called out, pausing the fighting for a brief moment. The vamp had taken Constance from his shoulder and now had her in his arms, her neck on full display and his fangs mere centimetres from puncturing her skin.

"Step back now or I bite her. And we all know how much your females enjoy our bite." The bastard was smirking and had Dominic shaking with rage. In that moment, he knew he would do anything for Constance.

"You wouldn't." Dominic called his bluff. "Whoever wants her will kill you if he knows you have tasted her first."

"He doesn't care," the vamp answered, licking his way up her neck. "He's going to let us all have a go."

The vamp straightened and pulled a small gun from his pocket. "But I will shoot her if you don't back the fuck up."

Dominic stood his ground. The vamp had to be bluffing. They wouldn't make the effort to break into the mansion if they meant her any harm.

"You are outnumbered, so I suggest you let the female go and we can then discuss how fast you want to die."

Surprisingly, instead of answering, instead of turning the gun on Constance, the vamp turned the gun on them.

"Fuck you," was all the vamp said as he emptied the gun on the enforcers and his own men. Dominic dived behind the vamp whose throat he still had a hold of and felt him jerk as a bullet hit him in the chest.

The shooting quickly stopped. The gun being small meant there weren't many bullets. Dominic peeked over the vamp he held and watched as the third ran down the corridor. Dominic leapt up to follow, only to be held back by Sebastian.

"What the fuck! Get off me."

"Dom, wait," Sebastian shouted, and pointed to small egg-shaped item that was slowly rolling down the corridor.

"Oh fuck! Move, move, move!"

All the enforcers dived for cover as the small grenade stopped between the two vamps. Time slowed as they looked at each other, before a flash of light sparked as the grenade exploded, taking them out.

29

_____

Accomplishments

MICHAEL WAS PLEASED. WHO WOULDN'T BE WHEN THEIR PLAN worked? The only thing that had put a dampener on his mood was now the hole that had taken a chunk out of the corridor, thanks to the vampyre's grenade. He had heard and felt the shock of that. He also was a little bit annoyed that Dominic hadn't been killed in the blast—or any of the other alphas. That would have helped a lot in ensuring his control over the race.

Now all he had to do was make sure the vampyre kept to his end of the deal, making sure the female didn't survive and then blame it all on the enforcers. The race would demand action, the alpha team would be disbanded, and its members punished. The race would turn to him yet again, and he would lead them. They would bow to him and he would be finally made King.

That was all he had ever wanted. The race to see him as he saw himself. A true leader. He would willingly sacrifice anyone to reach his goal. The queen and her consort had been the first of many, their daughter and her little protectors being the latest.

Michael smiled and lifted his crystal glass. The amber liquid sloshed as he saluted the portrait hung on the wall. The queen and her male looked back at him, judgement in their painted eyes.

"Here's to you and your pathetic offspring. Thank you for showing me that I am worth more than just a councillor."

He loved keeping the portrait. It reminded him of the things he had done and his goal. He was better than all of them put together. They had never deserved the throne. That was why he had conspired to have them removed. It was why he tolerated the vampyres. They were a means to an end, and even if it cost him the blood of many succubi females, he would be king.

A knock on the door had him smiling. It was time to act once again, but this would be the start of the end.

"Enter."

Two enforcers, neither one a member of the alpha team, ran into the room. They didn't bow, which annoyed Michael.

Soon they would learn.

"Yes?"

"My lord, there has been a breech in security. Three vampyres made it into the mansion."

"What? How is this possible?" He faked his outrage. Now it was time to plant the seed.

"What of the alphas? They should have prevented this."

"That is not all, my lord. The queen... she has been taken."

"No! Not the queen. What is being done?" Michael wanted to laugh, wanted to luxuriate in his victory. Instead, his face only showed worry and concern.

"The alphas responded, only the vampyre used a grenade. Dominic is going after her as we speak. They will not get away with this."

Michael nodded and sat back down from where he had jumped up in his fake outrange. He nodded at the two males.

"Thank you for informing me. I will let the council know," he stated, and waited for the males to turn before he continued.

"Gentlemen, I blame the alphas for this betrayal. As soon as your precious leader, Dominic, returns, I want him arrested. He has failed far too many times now for this to be ignored."

Both males looked at him with wide eyes, but neither questioned him. Instead, they nodded and left the room. Lifting his phone, Michael called his own guard. It had taken years to gain the loyalty of a select few males, making them see that his way was the only way. They would not only do anything he ordered but would kill on command.

It was time for the enforcers to retire. Permanently.

30

Blood Donor

CONSTANCE WOKE WITH A START. HER FACE THROBBED LIKE A bitch, especially her nose. She wouldn't be surprised if it was broken given how hard that bastard had hit her. Sitting up, Constance instantly groaned. The speed in which she did made her feel dizzy and she had to take deep breaths in and out through her nose to stop herself being sick.

She had been expecting to be in a cell or a cage, or something equally nasty, but instead found herself laying on a four-poster bed. It also had crimson, satin sheets, which made her want to roll her eyes. It was like something out of a cheesy romance, only this one didn't look like it was going to end with Constance being swept off her feet by the hero.

No, instead she was chained to one of the bed posts, her left hand now sporting a silver manacle with a matching chain that was hooked up to the post. The bed itself was beautifully carved in a deep mahogany and had matching crimson, velvet curtains. The bed was a masterpiece and was the kind you found in an old house. The curtains limited her view of the room, making her only able to see a large fireplace and the large chair that sat in front of it.

Constance tugged on the manacle, growling when nothing happened. No movement or give. The inside of it had been layered with cushioning so she didn't hurt herself. Obviously, her captor liked to keep his prisoners in comfort. Constance didn't like it and would have preferred to be kept in a cell. At least then she would know where she stood. Sliding herself up the bed, Constance lay against the cushions. Ways to try and escape entered her brain only to leave it just a swiftly as she realised they wouldn't work. Especially with the way she was now dressed.

Some cheeky git had changed her clothes whilst she had been unconscious. Gone was her hoodie and jeans, and now, she was dressed in a long white nightgown, with thick straps and ruffles.

Constance snorted. Yes, very much like a cheesy period romance book. The material was silk and felt amazing against her skin, but she hated feeling all exposed.

Other than the punch to the face, she was relatively unharmed—annoyed, but unharmed—and she wanted to keep it that way. She had been taken from her home and she had no idea why, but she would be dammed if she wasn't going back. She needed to sort things with Dominic.

Her heart leapt as she thought of him, hoping deep inside that he knew of her being missing and was coming after her.

"Ah, our guest is awake." The new voice broke through Constance's thoughts. The deep, gravelly sound of it made her curious. Who was it that had captured her, and why?

"Who's there?"

"Your host, my dear. I do hope you are comfortable?"

Constance raised an eyebrow and looked down at her new fashion accessory before she lifted the chain. "Really? Comfortable, is that what this is for?" She paused and wiggled the chain so it made a noise as she waited for the owner of the voice to come into view. "Learn something new every day."

A snort answered her, only to be followed by deep laughter as her host walked past the curtain to stand at the end of the bed.

Constance was unable to hold back a gasp. The male was stunningly beautiful. He had long brown hair teamed with an aristocratic face, full lips, and soulful eyes of deep blue. He wore fitted trousers and a white shirt with ruffles that opened up to reveal a well-defined chest. Constance, for a second, was enthralled, but that was all. Constance would not be distracted from the fact she had been kidnapped and was now chained to a bed. No matter how good-looking her captor was. Plus, as she looked her fill, he didn't measure up to Dominic.

His chest wasn't as big, neither were his arms, and his eyes weren't a bright green. He would be sadly mistaken if he thought he could make her forget the male who had her heart.

"Like what you see, female?" The male smirked and slowly slipped the shirt from his shoulders, revealing muscles and smooth skin. Maybe for another woman, this approach would work, but not for her.

"Listen, princess, how about you put your shirt back on and be a peach and let me out of this." She again picked up the chain and shook it. She would have laughed at the shock on the male's face at her answer, but his face soon changed from shock to pissed off.

"Insolent female," he growled. "I was told you were difficult."

"Who the hell are you and why have you kidnapped me?" she questioned. "And why have you changed my clothes? Where are my jeans?" The questions popped out of her mouth with no room for breath in between.

"Silence," the male shouted as he rounded the bed. It was like he glided instead of walked. "You are my honoured guest, my dear," he purred as he climbed onto the bed. "We treat succubi females well, so don't be alarmed."

"Right... Somehow I don't quite believe you," she said warily as she scooted away from the male. "Who are you?"

"Ahh yes, I am sorry. My name is Gabriel—Master, to my subjects," he answered as he smiled, flashing the biggest set of fangs she had ever seen.

"You're a... vampyre?" Flashbacks of her previous attack hit Constance hard; the pain, the feeling of her life being drained.

"Oh yes, dear, I am The Vampyre, and you belong to me." His fingers reached out and stroked up her neck. Dampness she had realised was there, was smoothed across her skin. "You will soon come to enjoy my touch, just as I enjoyed your taste."

The dampness, she now realised, was her blood. This male had already bitten her.

"They say it only takes a few bites for a succubi female to become addicted, to become aroused by it and then, in turn, beg for it. Shall we see how many it takes you?" He grasped her neck in a firm hold, one she couldn't break no matter how hard she tried. She didn't want his mouth anywhere near her, didn't want his bite, and most definitely did not want to get aroused by it.

"Fuck you," Constance grated out as she felt his tongue sweep up her neck, collecting the blood that had seeped from the wounds already present.

"Oh, sweetheart, don't worry. Soon you will beg me to do that as well." Between one breath and the next, he struck, his large fangs sinking into her flesh. There was no pleasure, only gut-ripping pain. Constance screamed in agony as he took her blood. Her fists thumped against his shoulder and the bed before sweet oblivion took over. Sending her into a pain-free darkness.

Sebastian sat in the office of the enforcers and eyed the alphas. Everyone but Dominic was present. All shared the same look as him.

Their queen had been kidnapped and their leader, Dominic, had gone off solo style to save her. They had all wanted to go, but Dominic had made them stay, stating he needed them. What worried Sebastian most was what would happen to Dom should he not be in time to find Constance.

Sebastian himself knew the pain of the losing a mate, knew it and had embraced the pain. Using that pain to help him be a better warrior. Dominic and Constance were two halves of one soul—that had been obvious by their blatant attraction to each other. He also hadn't missed Dominic scratching at his palms.

There was no other male more worthy of a female than Dominic, but now, Sebastian, for the first time in his long existence, wasn't sure what to do. His order to stay behind whilst their leader risked everything didn't sit well.

He looked at each of the men in turn before nodding. "Cooper, you know what to do. The rest of us will do as Michael asks. We know he's up to something, and as much as it makes me twitch to admit it, Dom was right. Michael is dangerous, so watch your backs."

"What about this order to arrest Dom?" Alec piped up, his phone in his hand as he monitored his surveillance systems.

"Ignore it," Sebastian stated clearly. "We swore our loyalty to our queen and to Dominic."

All the men nodded. Cooper stood from his chair and placed his hand over his chest.

"My brothers," he said seriously. "See you on the flip side." He smirked and left.

Sebastian knew Cooper would be stocking up on weapons and would go after Dominic. He was the best tracker out of them all, and if Dom struggled to find Constance, Cooper would be able to do it.

"Why did Dom go on his own? He knows he have his back. It's suicide," Alec argued. All of them had been a little put out when Dominic had gone on his own.

"He believes Constance to be his to protect and no one else's." Sebastian paused. "She's also his mate."

All nodded again. They didn't shock easily, and they had all known something had been up with their leader.

"So, what now?" Stefan asked, standing and starting to pace. The idea that they wouldn't fight meant they had a little bit more pent up energy and no way to siphon it off.

"We wait. Callum, take Helena to the royal wing. Now it is open, there is a possibility that Queen Ena left something that may help us."

"On it." Callum left quickly.

"The rest of us will wait to hear word from Dom,

because when he comes back—and he will—shit will go down."

Stefan grinned, Alec nodded, and Sebastian cracked his neck.

They hated waiting.

31

Freedom or Bust

The gentle strokes against her head brought Constance around. The soothing action almost lulled her back to sleep, but she fought it, pushing against the darkness to wake up. She had one goal:

Escape.

The master—or Gabriel—lay next to her, humming as he ran his fingers against her scalp, his eyes staring at the canopy above them. Constance didn't recognise the tune, but its sound was pleasant to the ear.

"I know you are awake." His voice was slow, almost like he was on the edge of sleep. "I'm sorry if I took too much, but you taste so damn good."

"Is that so?" Constance felt groggy. Her body wanted her to curl up and go back to sleep, but she couldn't afford to. Her only concern was getting away. That and fighting a possible addiction.

"How many times have you bitten me?" she asked as she slowly slid her lower body towards the edge of the bed.

"Mmm, three... maybe four... I lost count," his voice slurred.

"Right," she answered, still moving away from the male. She didn't feel any different. She wasn't screaming for his bite. In fact, she felt the opposite. Nausea and revulsion were the only things she felt at the thought of him biting her again.

"I want to bite you again, but... you need your rest," the male continued. At first, when Constance had seen him, she had thought he was this all-powerful leader, but now he was nothing more than an addict. No care for anything else but his next hit. Only, he wouldn't be getting one.

His gentle snores made her pause. This was her chance. Sliding her body and her hair free, Constance managed to manoeuvre herself off the bed. The chain rattled slightly, making her freeze.

Her captor lay like an Adonis on his back, muscles gleaming in the light. Ruined by his wide-open mouth and trail of drool.

"Big almighty leader, my arse." Constance snorted as she started to investigate the manacle and the chain that held her captive. Yet, no matter how hard she tugged, all the ways she tried to slide her hand out of the manacle, nothing worked.

"There has got to be a key," she commented out loud. Gabriel was flat out and couldn't hear her over his snores. As she eyed him on the bed, she tilted her head, ideas filtering into her mind.

"I wonder..." Slipping back onto the bed, careful to not wake Sleeping Beauty, Constance gently ran her hand up the leg nearest, feeling for pockets and a possible key. Only, there was nothing. His trousers were that tight she would have been able to see a slight bulge. Although she couldn't miss the bulge in the middle. This male did nothing for her, yet she had to nod in appreciation. He was packing.

Shaking her head, Constance slid closer. She had to check the other side, and that would mean leaning over Gabriel.

Holding her breath, she reached over, her eyes on him to make sure he didn't wake as she felt for a key in his pockets. Gabriel may not have opened his eyes—the male didn't need to, for as soon as Constance had finished checking his pockets, she found a hand in her hair.

"Mmm, time for another bite." His voice again held a husky edge. "You smell so delicious." The hand in her hair was stronger than she was, forcing her neck towards his gleaming fangs.

Constance smacked at his chest, but it didn't work. She dreaded his touch, shivered in disgust as he swept a tongue up her neck and scraped his fangs over the already opens wounds. Constance didn't want this. Tears filled her eyes as despair at not being able to get away filled her.

"I hate you," she sobbed. "I hate you." His fangs pierced her skin.

"Get your fucking fangs out of my female."

Dominic's rage fuelled him, everything else he sent to the back of his mind. Regardless of the reputation of vampyres, they had become a lazy race, feeding off only those weaker than them. Preferring to live in drug-filled stupors than be a race of worth. Yes, when enraged they could be fierce opponents, but nothing would stand in his way of getting his female back.

The guard at the entrance to the portal had nearly wet himself in fear when he had appeared through the doorway. Dominic didn't need to look into a mirror to see his eyes had now turned completely red and his fangs, that had been small, were now cutting into his lower lip.

His other side wanted out.

That same vampyre that had pissed himself became quite compliant and quickly gave up the information he needed. It had irked him that Cooper had caught up with him so quickly. Ideally, he needed the team back at the mansion to ensure Michael didn't do something stupid. But then again, that male only thought of himself and power, and would do the most ridiculous things to get it. Like have the new queen kidnapped and taken by vampyres, knowing what their bite would do.

Dominic's heart stuttered at the thought of a vamp feeding from Constance. The idea that another male would be touching what was his ramped his rage up another notch.

"So, what's the plan?" Cooper asked as they stood by a wall that marked the boundary to the vampyres main villa. Each race was housed in a different zone of Helvetia, with only the portals as entrances. Ideal. Even with a truce they would still try to hurt each other. It was politics. No race liked the vampyres due to the fact they had a tendency to kidnap other races' females as their own were now few and far between. The fae hated the weres, the succubi hated the demons, and so on.

"We need in, and we need in now," Dominic said impatiently.

"What about your..." Cooper wiggled his fingers.

"My what? What was that?" Dominic growled.

"Your superpowers. Where you blow shit up."

Dominic raised an eyebrow and turned to look at the entrance. No guards were posted so there may not be any need to blow anything up. Since his other side had been making a stir, his powers had been unstable. By trying to blow the doors open, he could take out the whole building and, in turn, risk Constance. That was out of the question.

"We go in the front door."

"What, as in walk up and ring the bell?" Cooper asked, frowning.

"Don't ring the fucking bell, just break down the goddamn door," Dominic snapped, and took off, his booted feet hitting the stone. In three strides he had cleared the steps that led to the entrance. Lifting his right leg, he kicked the solid wooden door and grinned when it flew off its hinges.

"See. Easy."

"Where is everyone?" Cooper asked, sliding a long blade from under his jacket.

Dominic ignored Cooper's question. Instead, he stepped to the side, letting Cooper go first.

"Do you think you can track her here?" Dominic asked.

Cooper nodded as he lifted his head, then tilted it. Dominic had always found it fascinating how the male tracked. It was like he had an internal radar that could be tuned into a single person's location. As much as his cocky attitude pissed some of the team off, his skills were irreplaceable.

He was their very own bloodhound. Only the male hated being referred to as one.

"I've got her," Cooper mentioned as he again tilted his head. Dominic clenched his fists again. His body hummed with the need to move, but he had to show some sort of patience.

With no other words, Cooper moved on. They both passed through an ornately decorated hallway, no expense spared from the way the gold gleamed from the marble. Yet even Dominic could tell it was falling apart. Pieces of stone and marble and gold dust littered the floors. This wasn't just the degradation of time; this was neglect.

The proud and noble warriors that were the vampyre race were no more. They had traded honour and pride for their own selfish gains. A part of Dominic was dismayed at this. To see a fellow immortal race succumb to the guilty pleasures of the modern world, to watch them fall so far... It gave a hint to what could happen to his own race if Michael was left to rule it.

Dominic focused on the male in front. Clutching his own daggers, he was on edge, expecting an attack to come from anywhere. The fact that the mansion was so quiet, worried him. The vamps he had faced in the past had always been game for a fight.

"Cooper?" he questioned, concerned they were in the wrong place completely. What if they were too late, and they had moved Constance? He felt the growl bubble up from within.

"She's here," was all Cooper said, yet he quickened his pace, his steps turning into a jog. No longer caring for stealth, the worn carpet did little to mask the sounds of their steps. A large wooden door loomed up ahead and Cooper slowed.

"This is it. She's in there."

Dominic nodded, taking in a deep breath. Finally, he was able to pick up her scent. The one that had pulled him to her from the beginning. Tinged within was a hint of fear. Dominic looked at the large door, knowing it would take more than a booted foot to open it. The wood was sturdy and would either need a key or an explosion. One he would have to risk.

Dominic closed his eyes and attempted to settle himself. It was hard when all he wanted to do was burst into that room and get to his female. He focused on the power he held deep within. It answered his call immediately. It swelled within his chest, and he felt his hands tingle in response. Only a hand on his shoulder stopped him from releasing it.

"The doors are unlocked," Cooper said, although he sounded just as surprised as he was. Nothing felt right with this raid. It was too easy. Stalking forward, he pushed open the door. The room was decorated in crimson and golds. His gaze searched and found his reason for living.

His Constance, his female... Only, a vampyre had his fangs in her neck.

"Get your fucking fangs out of my female," he growled out, and stalked forward. He hadn't missed the sobs of his female or her quiet pleas of hatred. He wanted to pull her away, take her in his arms, but he couldn't risk the bastard ripping her throat out. Only, as he approached, he recognised the male.

"Gabriel, you fucking arsehole." Dominic's growls grew louder. The leader of the vampyre race had indeed fallen. He had been well respected, only now he was nothing more than a junkie. This was why the palace had no guards, no locked doors, and no security. They were all either too high or had decided they didn't want to stay and follow a leader who would rather get lost in oblivion than lead.

There would be no fight, but death... Yes. What this male had done to his female alone warranted Dominic ending the pathetic creature's life. But Dominic's other side wouldn't get the fight he craved.

The male could barely keep his eyes open. The quiet snores told Dominic that Gabriel had fallen asleep and had released Constance. He could no longer hear her sobs, and that concerned him. Placing a knee onto the bed, he reached out and pulled her into the cradle of his arms, her light weight easy to lift as he took her from the bed and moved her away from the vampyre.

"Cooper, secure our passed out friend, will you, and see if you can wake him. I want answers before he dies."

"Yes, sir," Cooper answered as Dominic turned. With Constance in his arms, he felt centered again. What he had felt when they had been apart could only be described as not being able to draw a full breath. Her presence meant he could breathe again.

Stalking out the door, he walked to another, smaller one. Using his booted foot, he kicked it open, pleased to find another bedroom. One where he could look over his female. Gently setting her on the covers, concern mounted with every moment she didn't stir.

Her neck was red and swollen, puncture wounds present from multiple bites. Some cleanly done and some that were more like tears. His female had been used. Badly.

Stroking his hand over her skin—skin that was now so pale it was almost translucent—he found her pulse weak and breaths shallow. He expected her to wake up with red eyes much like his own, and to be an addict as all the stories in the past stated. A succubi female fed from multiple times by a vamp would become addicted to the bite. It was something he dreaded to see, but would fight with everything he had.

"Constance," he called out. Nothing.

Dominic started to panic. The vamp had taken too much of Constance's blood. She was dying.

"No! Not today and definitely not on my watch," Dominic shouted. "You are *mine,* Constance. *My* female. You will not leave me when I've just found you." He knew what he had to do. It was something he had wanted to do since his first moment with her, only he hadn't deemed himself good enough.

She was his to protect, his to love... *His.* He would do anything and everything for her.

Dominic lifted his wrist. Using his new, longer fangs, he bit deep, blood swelled immediately. Quickly, before his own body's healing gifts closed the wound, he placed it at Constance lips, forcing them open.

"Come on, sweetheart. Take it," he begged, using his other hand to massage her throat. His blood would not only save her life, but it would also seal the bond between them. She had tasted him before, but it was only a small cut from his lip. This was different.

Dominic was starting the ritual that would seal them as mates.

Slowly, he felt her respond. Her throat moved, swallowing the blood he had forced into her.

"That's it. Take it, baby. Take it all," he whispered, pleased when she gripped his arm to her mouth and started to suck. Each pull sent a bolt of lust to his groin. Dominic couldn't help but groan.

All too soon, she released his arm, yet her eyes stayed closed. Her breaths were deep, and her pulse was strong.

"Dominic?" Her gentle voice made him smile. No sign of addiction yet, but he would monitor the situation himself to see if it manifested itself at a later time.

"Yes, I'm here. Rest now." He smoothed her hair back from her face, unable to stop himself from touching her.

"Don't leave."

"Never," he answered as he took her within his arms again, pleased when she snuggled into his embrace. This was it, right here. Why the world spun. Why life began. It was for love. Yes, he loved Constance. She was the air he breathed, and he would love her until his last breath.

32

Time to Play

COOPER SAT ON ONE OF THOSE PUFFED UP LUXURIOUS armchairs and admired his handiwork. Dominic had ordered him to deal with the vamp, and he thought he had done a damn good job. The high as fuck vamp was now hanging upside down from the top of the posts of the four-poster bed he had been lounged on. All Cooper had to do now was wait for the arsehole to wake up, and judging by the way his face was becoming a bright shade of red, it wouldn't be long now.

So, he sharpened his knife as he waited. He used to be like Dom and his other alphas, using two smaller daggers. But after seeing a certain film, he had taken to using one super-long and large-ass blade. He found it was more effective, both in action and as a deterrent.

Mr fucking Dundee had sweet FA on this blade. As much a Cooper looked forward to a good torture session, he was just as eager as Dominic to get back to the mansion. The small female they had rescued was currently being watched over by their healer.

She had been on his mind since he had found her. Her pleas of death hadn't sat right, and Cooper found himself desperate to learn more about her. She had been beautiful when they had freed her from the facility. But once she had been cleaned up, Cooper had found it hard to speak. She was an angel.

Shaking his head, Cooper stood. He was fed up of waiting, and waiting only led to his mind going to mush over a female he had no right to think about. Taking his blade, which he had nicknamed Boris the Blade, he twirled it in his hand and squatted down.

"Wakey, wakey, princess, come and meet Boris," he cooed as he slid the tip of the blade down the male's sternum, belly to throat. A thin line bloomed in seconds. Not deep enough to count, but it would hurt none the less. A groan erupted from the male's mouth, yet he still didn't wake. The fact the male still had his queen's blood around his mouth pissed Cooper off.

This male had abused one of their females, and as Dominic had stated, he would die. But not before he found out how the male had got his little bitches into their home and who had helped him.

"Come on, fucker, I don't have all day to play with you," Cooper growled, and sliced the male again, this time across, from left to right.

This time the groan was louder, and as the male opened his eyes, Cooper was there.

"Good morning, sunshine." He grinned.

"Who the hell are you?" The male, also known as

Gabriel, leader of the vampyres, cried out as he realised he was upside down and, in short, fucked.

Cooper felt a little bit cliché with his answer, but he shrugged. It worked.

"Your worst fucking nightmare. Time to talk, sweetheart," he purred as he placed the blade to the vampyres bare chest yet again. The room was filled with the scent of blood. Cooper had a job to do, and he wouldn't let his leader, or queen, down.

33

The Bond had Begun

DOMINIC CARRIED HIS SLEEPING MATE FROM THE BEDROOM they had borrowed. She had fed and was now healing nicely. Although Dominic was now plagued with itchy palms. He had hoped to see his bonding marks appear, yet nothing had.

Moving back towards the large door, the smell of fresh blood reached him. Not wanting to risk Constance seeing the carnage that was Cooper's fun time, he called out.

"Cooper, you all done in there?"

Unexpectedly, Cooper's face appeared around the edge of the door. The male looked quite happy.

"Everything ok? We need to get back."

"Yes, all is going well. But I'm not done," Cooper admitted. "I believe there is more to get from him, and he's being so well behaved."

Dominic raised an eyebrow. "Right. What has he told you so far?"

"Oh, that it was Michael who orchestrated the kidnapping and also was the one to allow the vamps into the mansion. It doesn't stop there though. Looks like our little fucknugget of a councilman had a hand in the deaths of the former queen and consort as well."

"Fuck," Dominic whispered, and pulled Constance closer to his body. "He really will not stop at nothing to keep power, will he?"

"That male is a wankstain on the carpet that is life," Cooper stated clearly, nodding.

"A different way to put it, but yes. That's why I need to get Constance back." Dominic continued, "Call Sebastian and let him know I'm on my way back. Stay here and find out what you can, but don't risk yourself, Cooper. I am going to need you back at the mansion."

"You got it, boss man. I won't be long." He grinned and pulled out his phone as Dominic turned away. He needed to get Constance back to the mansion. It was a lot to ask of her as she had already been through so much, but she needed to assert her power over the councilman and get him to back down. With her back, the alphas could finally take him out.

"Dom." Constance's voice pulled him from his thoughts.

"Hey there," he answered, and a lump caught in his throat as he looked down at her still too pale skin.

"You came for me?" she questioned, frown lines appearing between her eyes.

"Of course I did. Woman, I would defy death itself for you," he answered honestly, because he really didn't know what the future was to hold for them. He watched as Constance smiled and closed her eyes again, her whispered words filling his soul with light.

"I love you, Dom."

34

Be the Queen

CONSTANCE WOKE WITH A START. FLASHBACKS OF EVERYTHING that had happened whipped through her brain, giving her an instant headache. She expected to see crimson sheets and gaudy furniture, yet all she saw were the cream sheets of her own bed and a worried Helena sat on the end of it.

"My lady," she started to say, only was stopped by the flow of tears.

"Helena," Constance cooed, and held her arms open. Helena flew into them and hugged her tight.

"When I was told what had happened, I thought we would lose you. Thought you would become addicted, and then Michael would order you put down like he tried to do to me." She sobbed some more, and Constance just listened.

She didn't feel addicted. In fact, considering what she had been through, she felt strong and ready to take on the world.

"You are not addicted?" Helena asked, finally looking up, and Constance shook her head.

"The vampyre's bite was painful. Every time he did it, I hated it," she admitted. "I think he was the one addicted to me."

"That's good," Helena answered, and squeezed her hands. "I need to tell you what's been going on with Michael," she continued. "He's a nasty man, Connie," Helena stated. "He... he—he's arrested Dominic and has stated you are not fit to be Queen. He states that you have been compromised and has blamed everything on Dominic and the alphas."

"What?" Constance shouted. She had been disappointed to find Helena and not Dominic at her bedside. But she now understood why.

Helena continued, "He has his own enforcers who are loyal to only him, and he believes now that he will be crown king, especially if he can make the council see that you are not fit."

"That jumped up little shit," Constance growled out, and flung the covers back on the bed.

"I may not have been here long—hell, I may not know what the fuck I'm doing half the time—but I know I have you and the alphas here to help me. I will be fucked if I let some power-crazy dipshit ruin the lives of the people I care about and—" She paused. She was now stood in the middle of her large bedroom, hands on hips, dressed in only a pair of sleep shorts and a Garfield top. "And try to take my throne from me before I've even been crowned."

Moving through the room, she ignored the rustle of Helena's skirts as she tried to keep up with her.

"My mother saved my life by sending me away from the reach of that bell-end, so in the end, I could make the losses worth it and lead this race again." Her ranting had placed a smile on Helena's lips.

"So..." She grinned and walked towards the desk that was placed in a small office just off her bedroom. It was basically a small library with another huge fireplace and cosy chairs. She had found this place was where she could relax, surrounded by books. When she had been exploring, she had found a secret cupboard behind one of the walls, and it had been there she had discovered a few things left by her mother. Only, she hadn't really had time to read them. Except for a single letter.

She hadn't had chance to say anything to anyone about them before she was kidnapped, but now was the time to do just that. Opening the cupboard, she pulled out three items. A letter, a diary, and the one item she guessed she would need today. She mainly needed what it represented.

"This is a letter from my mother, stating that she didn't feel safe and, as such, sent me away with one of her ladies in waiting. The woman I have always known as my mother and who currently resides in St. Joseph's. My father was sent on a mission not long before, at the insistence of Michael, stating it was for the good of the race and was of the upmost importance. But it turned out to be a trap. One that led to my father's death. My mother knew this—I'm not sure how. Lives—not just my parents but others of the race—have suffered because of Michael."

Holding up the diary, she stepped close to Helena. "This diary holds within it all the information we need to stop Michael. My mother died because she lost her mate. I will not suffer the same fate," she stated clearly, and placed the third item she had pulled out on her head.

The golden crown sparkled in the light; diamonds, rubies, emeralds. Gemstones of all colours glittered, casting rainbow reflections across the room. "What do you think? Does this make me look like a queen?" Constance asked her friend, because that was what Helena was and what Constance had always wanted.

"My lady."

"Connie," Constance growled out, and grinned.

"Connie, the crown may make you a queen, but to make you a lady, we need to get you in a dress fit for the post. But we must hurry. I believe they are starting Dominic's trial soon."

Constance's heart stalled. She would need to muster every ounce of courage she had to take Michael head on. He would not take away her mate. Her love. Yes, she loved him. She had said it and she was sure of it.

Looking down, Constance watched as the marks on her hands darkened.

"What will they do to him?" Constance asked as Helena led her back into the bedroom and started laying out her queenly robes.

"I dread to think, my lady, but it won't be pleasant." Helena's voice caught.

"Has Callum been arrested too?" she asked, already knowing the answer.

"Yes, along with Sebastian, Alec and Stefan. Cooper had still not returned from the vampyre hold where they found you."

It wasn't just her own mate she had to worry about, but also Helena's. It was time for Constance to embrace her heritage, time to become the queen she was always destined to be. Time for her to show them that not all females need protecting, and not all females are pushovers.

"Right, let's do this. Tell me everything I need to know."

35

Worthy vs Unworthy

Dominic's nostrils flared. He was pissed. As soon as he had walked back through the portal, he had been arrested, his mate taken from his arms, and was cuffed.

Now, he was knelt in the council chamber, his arms strung above his waist as the councilmen—men of his race he had served loyally—looked on. His fellow alpha team were also cuffed and stood to the side, each one just as frustrated as he was. All of them shooting daggers at Michael, who had seated himself on the throne.

Whatever sway he had made with this council and the other enforcers was a lie. There was no way the men under his command would have turned on him as quickly as they did otherwise.

"My, how I do enjoy seeing you on your knees, Dominic," Michael taunted. "It's where you belong, after all."

"How about you release me and we see where *you* really

belong?" Dominic growled back, and tugged on the chains that held his arms.

"Tut, tut, that's no way to talk to your king, is it." Michael rose from the throne in one fluid motion, his robes billowing behind him.

"As you can see, my fellow councilmen, this enforcer shows no respect to his leader or superiors. He allowed our beloved queen to be taken. It is his fault that she has succumbed to the addiction of a vampyre's bite and, as such, is not fit to rule. The kindest thing we can do for her now would be to put out of her misery as soon as possible."

Dominic watched as he circled the room, spewing his lies, and growled. He wasn't sure if the male was, in fact, telling the truth with regards to Constance, but there was no way he would allow her to be killed, even if he was. He just needed out of these chains.

"It is a pity that one so young should be dealt with in this manner, but it must be done. As for the subject of succession, I believe it is time that we look to new blood to rule."

Dominic snorted. "New blood? Why don't you just tell them, Michael," Dominic taunted back, not at all afraid of the male. "You plan to rule. That was the intent all along, wasn't it?" Dominic questioned.

"You have no idea what you are talking about, you pathetic half-breed," Michael snapped, and gave fake a smile to the council.

"Really? So it wasn't your intent to have the queen's consort led into a trap and killed? And it wasn't your idea to have our new queen kidnapped in the hope she would die, or as you said, become addicted?"

Michael glared at Dominic, but he didn't stop. "You've

always wanted power, Michael. God forbid the true leader appearing to take it from you."

Michael glared again at Dominic, and then turned his back. Dominic watched the male as he circled the room again, before he stalked back to the throne, sitting on it like he belonged.

"Lies," he stated. "All lies."

"It is truth," Dominic countered.

"But where is your proof?" Dominic ground his teeth. He was wondering the same thing. Cooper had been tasked with that job and was still AWOL.

"See, there is none. Let us get on with the festivities, shall we. Dominic, you have been charged with treason to the succubi throne. Your sentence will be one hundred lashes, followed by a good old-fashioned beheading. How do you plead?"

The smirk on Michael's face enraged Dominic. He was not afraid to die. But he would not die a traitor.

"Where's the queen, Michael? Prove she's addicted and cannot take the throne. Or have you finally grown some balls and killed her yourself?" Inside, Dominic didn't believe Constance was dead, yet the mere thought of any harm to her ramped his other side's rage up a notch. Michael ignored his taunt, even though the council members had nodded at Dominic's suggestion.

"Begin with the punishment," Michael stated, and turned to the other alphas. "Do not worry, your turn is next."

Dominic looked at his fellow enforcers. They had served together for a long time and had a bond only made closer by blood.

"Die with honour." Sebastian, Callum, Alec and Stefan all bowed their heads before repeating the words back.

Dominic then faced Michael, his eyes on the male even as he felt his tormentor approach.

He heard the whoosh of leather through the air before pain erupted through his back, slicing through skin and hitting bone. Still, he didn't cry out. Instead, he watched Michael. With every strike, he watched as the male, who wanted to lead the race, flinch. Even as his blood flowed down his back, he didn't make a noise, didn't turn away.

Let Michael know this was what a real male did for his race. He would die for it and his queen, and he would die with honour.

～

Constance ran down the corridor, following Helena because Helena had been brought up within the mansion. She knew all the secret passageways that even Michael was unaware of.

"Connie, this corridor will lead us straight into the council chambers and behind the throne. I'm not sure what is happening. All the enforcers are there, and so is the council." Helena looked concerned as she held out her hand. In her palm lay a small dagger, its hilt richly decorated. "Take this, just in case."

"I can't accept that, honey." Constance wanted to hug her friend, but time was of the essence.

"Please," Helena insisted. "Give it back to me after, ok? And take this." She handed over a small torch. "The corridor is dark."

"Fine." Constance smirked and gave in, hugging her friend fiercely. "Wait in the royal suite, ok?"

Helena nodded before she ran back the way they had come. As much as she wanted the support, she didn't want

Helena anywhere near Michael. Not when he had ordered her death previously. She wouldn't put it past the male to try and make an example out of her.

Picking up her own skirts, Constance moved down the dark and unused corridor. Cobwebs littered the way, making her skin crawl—a clear sign no one had used this way since her mother had died. Her dress was of emerald green that was off the shoulder and had long sleeves. The skirts and petticoats meant it flared out, but it made her look the part. That, coupled with her new crown, Constance felt a little more like a queen than she did before.

As she moved onwards, she could make out the murmur of voices and other odd noises. She just hoped she wasn't too late.

Finding the door at the end, she used the torch to find the handle, hoping the hinges weren't rusted and give away her location.

Pushing through the door and moving the curtain that was in front of her, she stood partially hidden behind the throne. The room was filled, yet no one said a word now. Only a whoosh of something flying through the air before it hit something with a thwack could be heard.

Her nose itched as a delicious scent reached it. Moving out of the shadow of the curtain, she let it fall, hiding the way she had come in, and took a look at the scene displayed before her. Constance had to hold in the gasp that wanted to shoot out. Placing a hand against her mouth, she bit down on a finger.

The whoosh and thwack now made sense. Her male...

The man she had come to love was chained to a post and was being whipped. The scent she had found so delicious was his blood. Blood that now ran in streams down his body and pooled on the floor.

"Stop this at once," Constance shouted as she walked forward. Every single pair of eyes landed on her, even those of Dominic, but she couldn't lose focus. Not now.

"My lady." Michael's voice slid over her nerves and made her twitch. "You are fully healed, then?" he asked. Constance didn't try to hold beck her distain for the male. Instead, she embraced it.

"Clearly." She moved forward again and looked down at the male who had the nerve to sit in her seat. "Is there a reason you are in my seat, councilman?"

Constance could clearly see the rage in his eyes as he stood. There was zero respect there, as expected. Constance would have a fight on her hands, but it was worth it if she could free Dominic.

"I'm afraid there has been change of plans, my lady."

"Really? I wasn't aware of the original plans, so please enlighten me as to why you are, one, sat in my chair," she held up her fingers, physically ticking off the points, "two, why Dominic is chained and being whipped, and three, why my alphas are also chained up."

"They are being tried for treason," he admitted with a smirk.

"Really? Treason against who? Because they sure as hell haven't committed any treason against me. In fact, it was Dominic and his alphas who came to my rescue—for the second time."

She watched as the male walked away but didn't answer. Dread slivered up her neck.

Michael stopped near to Dominic. "This male will die for treason, my lady. Treason to the council."

"No, he will not," Constance argued, and stepped down onto the main floor to address the council members. Pulling back her sleeves, she held up the deep, dark marks on her hands.

"I believe you all recognise these." She slowly turned, showing them to all, even the alphas who, to her joy, grinned. Dominic himself said nothing, but his eyes widened.

"They are bonding marks, my lady," one member called out, followed by another.

"Who is the male?"

"When did this happen?"

"The male is more worthy than any of you councilmen." Constance let her anger out. "More honourable than you— men of power who have let out race become corrupt and easily swayed by power." She looked at Michael, pleased to see anger return to his eyes. His lip curled in disgust and he clenched his fists.

"My mate is Dominic, leader of the enforcers and alpha team. The male you are currently trying for treason with no evidence but the word of a male who cannot be trusted."

Constance walked over to Dominic, her eyes never leaving Michael. She didn't trust him and would rather not leave her guard open.

"Please release the queen's consort," she ordered, pleased to see the enforcer males move forward.

"Stop this," Michael screamed, and dived at Constance. "I rule. Not you!" His hand gripped her arm as he produced a small dagger. Hers was in the folds of her dress and out of reach. Constance fought, using all her strength to stop him from stabbing her.

"Enforcers, free the alphas," she screamed out, pleased when they all rushed to do her bidding. The cowardly councilmen shook in their seats, but Constance only had eyes for the dagger moving her way. Her arms shook with the effort of holding him away. He may not be as built as the enforcers, but he still had more strength than she did.

Constance felt the cold sharpness of steel as the blade sank an inch into the flesh of her stomach, Michael's evil grin holding her gaze. Yet all around were shouts of warning.

Those shouts were drowned out as an inhuman roar filled the room. One moment, Michael was winning, the next, she watched as he flew across the room, hitting a marbled pillar. His assailant, her male. Dominic stood in the centre of the room.

Constance gasped with shock, even as the pain from where Michael had stabbed her made her shake. Dominic had changed.

Bigger by two feet, Dominic was also wider, but the most noticeable difference was the wings. Black feathered wings unfurled. The wounds that had covered his back were gone, leaving only scars in their place. She watched as he turned to face her, his chest heaving and his now bright red eyes focused on the blood that seeped from her wound. Pain etched his face, but anger overtook it, and he turned back to the male who had caused so much damage.

"My lady, let us move you." Sebastian appeared. Reaching under her, he lifted her into his arms, yet she couldn't look away from Dominic. His wings dragged on the ground, creating a sweeping noise that, coupled with his growls, filled the room.

"What?" was all she could get out.

"He's a fallen, my lady. Rare, to say the least," Sebastian answered in awe. The rest of the alphas, now freed, circled her, protecting her when Dominic couldn't. Sebastian kept talking, helping her maintain some semblance of calm. "Fallen angel... He always knew he was a half-breed. I guess we now know what his other half is. They are one of the rarest of the immortals and almost invincible."

"He's one big fucker, isn't he," Cooper's voice called out from the back as he moved forward.

"Where the fuck have you been?" Sebastian growled. "We could have done with you a while back."

"I had a situation with one pissed off vamp. All good though—and I'm ok. Thanks for asking."

Constance watched Sebastian glare at the male before they all turned back to watch Dominic work.

Michael had enlisted some of his own enforcers who now faced off with Dominic, protecting the male they thought would lead them to greatness but instead would only lead them to death.

"Should we... you know, help?" Alec asked as an enforcer was thrown across the room, headfirst into the wall. Dead on impact.

"Do you want to get between Dom and them? Really?" Cooper replied.

"Err... no. He was a mean son of a bitch before he went super Hulk on us," Alec answered, and Constance had never felt more at home than she did in that moment. Surrounded by the alphas and watching her male seek retribution.

36

Royally Fallen

DOMINIC FELT POWER, RAW AND UNTAMED, AS HE LET HIS other side free, no longer caring about consequences. Watching the female he loved fight for her life had been it for him. Watching as that cowardly bastard pushed a blade into her flesh had released the lock he had put down on the side of him he knew nothing about.

The roar he released erupted from his mouth, and at the same time, he felt his back rip open.

"What the fuck are you?" Michael screamed as he picked him up by the back of his neck and threw him across the room, away from his mate.

Mate... Her words declaring him her consort had hit him in the heart. The pain of the whipping had been forgotten as he had watched his magnificent mate take on Michael. Dominic should have known the male wouldn't give up.

Now it was his turn to protect his female, his queen. Turning his head, he looked down at her, eyeing the wound that was bleeding freely. He would kill for her, starting with the male who had caused her pain. The fangs that filled his mouth stopped any speech, but he could still growl.

Somehow, Michael had gained the loyalty of a few enforcers, and it was them who stood in front of him now, keeping Dominic away from his quarry. As one dived at him with a blade, he caught him with the back of his hand, sending the male sailing into the other wall. Hitting it head on, it killed him instantly.

He snarled at the three remaining males. His fingers now sported claws that could take a head clean from its shoulders, and that's what he planned to do.

He had heard Sebastian's words to Constance. He knew what he was, and he embraced it. Blood coated him from head to toes as he ripped apart the three enforcers, their bodies thrown to the way side as he stalked the now petrified Michael.

The rest of the councilmen had fled once they witnessed what Dominic was capable of. He would deal with them another time. He pointed at the male, his word slurred due to the fangs.

"You," was all he said, and he watched as the male wet himself. He sneered in repulsion. He had a task to do.

Taking the male by the throat, he lifted him and turned, facing the enforcers and his alpha team. There, in his second's arms, was his mate, and he looked to her for permission. She was still Queen, and he lived for her.

Michael squirmed in his hold, his eyes wide with fear in knowing his death was coming. Death was too good for the male, but he couldn't be allowed to live, not when he had caused so much death to the succubi race and the royal family.

His eyes met those of Constance's. He expect fear but instead found acceptance. Her eyes crinkled slightly as she smiled, but they turned cold as she looked at the male in his grip. With no pause, she nodded, already knowing what he was asking permission for.

Turning, he took the male away from his mate. He didn't want her to watch. Didn't want her to see him kill. But he also knew she would want to watch. To see justice for her parents carried out.

"Please... don't kill me. I will do anything!" Michael cried out as Dominic set him on the floor but didn't release him. He felt the presence of his alpha team at his back. A quick turn of his head and he saw his queen on her throne, Sebastian, Cooper, Alec, Callum and Stefan at his side. The other enforcers circled the room. Watching and waiting.

Constance's voice filled the air.

"Michael, you are charged with treason against the throne of the succubi race for the murder of the queen's consort and, in turn, the death of the queen. You are also charged with the attempted murder of the new queen. How do you plead?"

Michael said nothing, only whimpered as his eyes flicked from one face to another, searching for help. Only, he would receive none.

"Thought so. Your sentence is death," Constance stated coldly.

With one sweep of his claw, Dominic sliced through Michael's throat, almost taking his head clean off. His body hit the deck immediately as his life's blood pooled beneath him to join that of the dead enforcers. It was a bloody way to die, but it was the succubi way.

Turning, he looked up at Constance and felt his other

side shrink back, his wings folding and vanishing into his back. His eyes meeting hers, he dropped to one knee, followed by every other male in the room.

"Hail Regina!"

37

Rest is for the Weak

"WOMAN, YOU ARE SUPPOSED TO BE IN BED," DOMINIC'S VOICE called from the bedroom as soon as he found her out of the bed. She had snuck into the office and was curled up in what was her mum's favourite chair, reading her diary and getting to know her parents the only way she could.

Yes, yesterday had been a bloody mess. Literally. But she was healing quickly thanks to Dominic's fallen blood that ran through her veins. Yet Dominic seemed intent on keeping her bedbound. The love she felt for her male was wildly intense. Her marks were now solid black, although Dom's were still faint. At first, she found this worrying, but Sebastian had thought it was something to do with his fallen status.

Sebastian had also been able to answer why she had not succumbed to addiction as well. Dominic had already bitten her when they had first partially bonded, so his bite was a lot more potent than a vampyres. Constance had smiled when she had been told, knowing that it was her mate all along who had protected her, even when he wasn't there.

"Constance. Come on, baby, you should be resting," Dominic called from the doorway, and Constance couldn't help her breath catching as she looked up at him. He was dressed in black, as all the enforcers did, but he had yet to put his shirt on, leaving him gloriously bare-chested and free for her to perv on.

"I am resting," Constance argued, but like a spoilt child, she held her arms up, knowing her male would collect her and carry her to bed. She had just read something written by her mother and wanted to try it out.

Constance heard Dominic's chuckle as he stepped into the room and moved to her chair, quickly gathering her in his arms.

"Lazy wench," he whispered against her ear as he nuzzled the skin just below it, making her shiver in delight.

"That's Queen Lady Wench to you," she playfully argued as she wrapped her arms around his neck, refusing to let go as he laid her down, their mouths only breaths apart. She felt the touch of his lips on hers, and gave in to the kiss, loving the way he caged her body in with his own.

"Dominic," she called as his lips left hers and travelled down her neck. "Dom," she called again. She was a bag of nerves. He was her mate, yet she was scared of rejection.

"Heart of my heart,
Soul of my soul,
Together as one,
Always whole.
This male I take as my bonded,
This male I take as my own.
Bond us together for all time,
Always together, never alone."

Dominic had paused as she started the words of the bonding ritual, his eyes widening as he realised what it was she was saying. After she had recited that last part, she waited.

"Truly?" he asked.

Constance nodded and smiled. Reaching under her pillow, she collected a small dagger.

Dominic swooped down to feast on her lips, leaving her breathless before he pulled away and took the dagger from her hand.

"Heart of my heart,
Soul of my soul,
Together as one,
Always whole.
This female I take as my bonded,
This female I take as my own.
Bond us together for all time,
Always together, never alone."

Taking the dagger, Dominic slid the blade across his left palm before he took Constance's right hand. Before slicing hers, he kissed her palm gently, his eyes never leaving hers.

She felt the cool metal and a brief hint of pain. Constance pressed her bleeding palm to Dominic's, interlocking their fingers as they both recited the last part of the ceremony.

"Bonded with blood, bonded with love. By the gods', will let this be done."

Constance felt her body respond—as it always did with Dominic nearby—only this time it was like she could feel the pull to him through her very soul.

"Can you feel that?" she asked breathlessly. "I can feel you." She was awed, not only by her own feelings for

Dominic but also by the fact she could feel the intensity of what he felt for her.

"Yes," he breathed back, and took her lips in a quick, brutal kiss. "I feel you. All of you," he whispered, before he pulled back to look into her eyes again. She felt his hands as they stroked her face.

"You are mine."

"As you are mine," she answered, and grinned. She groaned at the look of intense desire that filled his gaze.

"My queen." He kissed her lips.

"My love." He kissed her again, but harder.

"My mate." Constance's groan was lost as he poured every ounce of love and possession into the kiss, fuelling her own desire. Hands glided over skin as Constance became lost to his touch, giving herself to the male who had become her world.

This male was all she would ever need. All she wanted.

Her consort.

Her love.

Her mate.

38

Dark Possession Book 3 Dark Desire Series

SEBASTIAN SAT IN THE OFFICE. IT WAS NOW HIS OFFICE AS Dominic had made the move into the royal suite. It felt a tad lonely without his friend, but he doubted he would be lonely for long. Not with the likes of Cooper and Alec.

Since the events in the council chamber, the whole race had been shaken by the depth of Michael's deceit. Now, it was up to their new queen, Constance, to fix the fuck ups he had made. But with the backing of the enforcers and with her mate and consort by her side, he was confident that things for the race were now looking up.

A knock at the door had Sebastian looking up. Cooper stood inside the door, a look of worry on his face.

"What's wrong now? Don't tell me you pissed someone else off again?" Sebastian asked, and stood, quickly moving around the desk. Cooper was a talented enforcer and alpha, but his issue was he couldn't keep his mouth shut. That alone got him into more scrapes than was normal.

"No, it's not me. You now I brought that vamp back for questioning, right?"

"Yeah, but you'd better not let Dom know you have him." Sebastian could see the logic behind why Cooper had brought him back and not killed him outright. Dominic wouldn't. As far as he was concerned, the male had harmed his mate, nearly drank her dry, and as such, Dominic would prefer it if the male was no longer breathing.

"I know but... well, our chats have revealed more information," Cooper started, the look of worry returned.

"And? What has he said?"

"He mentioned the fact that Michael had been supplying females to him for quite a while."

Sebastian remained quiet, his body going stock still.

"He knew them all by name and mentioned there were a few that had tried to escape," Cooper continued, although he seemed wary.

"One in particular, he remembered, was the only one to succeed. He had been gutted as she had 'tasted the sweetest to him'."

Sebastian growled as pain sharper than any knife erupted through his chest. His words came out as a snarl.

"Say it. Say her name!"

"Gabriel stated that Aria was the female to escape." Cooper's words caused Sebastian to fall to his knees as agony flowed through just as intense as it had been the day she was found missing. The day his mate and he should have had their bonding ceremony.

He had searched for her until he had been ordered back home for fear he would turn feral or perish through malnourishment. But she had been out there, alone and unprotected, and he had let it happen. Guilt weighed upon his shoulders.

She was his to protect...

He would find her.

ALSO BY J THOMPSON

Soulmate Series

SoulKiss-http://soulmatenovels.com/soulkiss.htm

SoulFate-http://soulmatenovels.com/soulfate.htm

SoulDeath-http://soulmatenovels.com/souldeath.htm

Dark Desire Series

Dark Confusion-http://soulmatenovels.com/dark-confusion.htm

Dark Need-http://soulmatenovels.com/dark-need.htm

Dark Possession-coming August 2021

Trinity Series

Ebony-http://soulmatenovels.com/ebony.htm

Paranormal Security Service

Guarding Katelyn-http://soulmatenovels.com/guardian-katelyn.htm

Tears of Havoc

Cupid's Essence-http://soulmatenovels.com/cupids-essence.htm

Elemental Dragons Series

Earth Dragon's Claim-http://soulmatenovels.com/earth-dragons-claim.html

Co-authored

Dragon fire and Phoenix Ash-http://soulmatenovels.com/dragon-fire-and-phoenix-ash.htm

Draakon Desire Series

Raanar-My Book

Stand Alones

Exercise in Love -http://soulmatenovels.com/exercise-in-love.htm

Magic and Mayhem Universe

Witch out of Water-Kracken's Hole Book 1-https://magicandmayhemuniverse.com/j-thompson/

Tail of a witch- Kracken's Hole Book 2-https://magicandmayhemuniverse.com/j-thompson/

Witch out of Luck- Kraken's Hole Book 3-https://magicandmayhemuniverse.com/j-thompson/

Altorian Cyborgs

Betraying Ko'ran- http://soulmatenovels.com/betraying-koran.htm

ABOUT THE AUTHOR

J. Thompson is a USA Today Bestselling Author of Paranormal and Sci-Fi romance and a major fan of procrastination. Jenn has always loved history, so using her wild imagination and tying in her love of history and fantasy, she began a new adventure into the world of words. Weaving romance into old worlds and giving life to her mythical inspired novels is what Jenn does best, and she has a lot more planned in the future, including some hard assed demons.

When she isn't bent over her laptop with the crazy writer eyes, you will find Jenn making jewellery, cross stitching and it doing paper crafts. Jenn is also an avid lover old skool skills like archery and sword fighting.

Maybe a touch nuts Jenn is an author who believes wholeheartedly that people are good and that everyone deserves romance - even Hades.

Connect with Jean online at www.soulmatenovels.com
For regular updates sign up to Jenns Newsletter HERE